Penguin Books
Penguin Modern Stories 7

D1426050

Penguin
Modern
Stories 7

Edited by Judith Burnley

Penguin Books

Penguin Books Ltd, Harmondsworth,
Middlesex, England
Penguin Books Australia Ltd, Ringwood,
Victoria, Australia

First published in book form in Great Britain by
Penguin Books 1971
'The Muse' copyright © Anthony Burgess, 1968, 1971
'In the Conservatory'; 'How Soon Can I Leave?'
copyright © Susan Hill, 1971
'Battle for the Hill'; 'Nina of Ashkelon'
copyright © Yehuda Amichai, 1967, 1971
'Instructions for the Use of Women'; 'For Bolocks
Please Read Blocks Throughout'; 'Mean Point of Impact'
copyright © B. S. Johnson, 1971

Made and printed in Great Britain by
C. Nicholls & Company Ltd
Set in Monotype Baskerville

Contents

Anthony Burgess   The Muse 7

Susan Hill   In the Conservatory 29

How Soon Can I Leave? 47

Yehuda Amichai   Battle for the Hill 61

Nina of Ashkelon 95

B. S. Johnson   Instructions for the Use of Women
or Here, You'veBeen Done 115

For Bolocks Please Read Blocks Throughout 123

Mean Point of Impact 129

Anthony Burgess

The Muse

'You're quite sure,' asked Swenson for the hundredth time, 'you want to go through with this?' His hands ranged over the five manuals of the instrument console and, in cross-rhythm, his feet danced on the pedals. He was a very old man, waxed over with the veneer of rejuvenation chemicals. Very wise, with a century of experience behind him, he yet looked much of an age with Paley, the twenty-five-year-old literary historian by his side. Paley grinned with un-diminished patience and said:

'I want to go through with it.'

'It won't be quite what you think,' said Swenson. (This too he had said many times before.) 'It can't be absolutely identical. You may get shocks where you least expect them. I remember taking Wheeler that time, you know. Poor devil, he thought it was going to be the fourteenth century he knew from his books. But it was a very different four-teenth century. Thatched cottages and churches and manors and so on, and lovely cathedrals. But there were poly-cephalic monsters running the feudal system, with tentacles too. Speaking the most exquisite Norman French, he said.'

'How long was he there?'

'He was sending signals through within three days. But he had to wait a year, poor devil, before we could get him out. He was in a dungeon, you know. They got suspicious of his Middle English or something. White-haired and gibbering when we got him aboard. His jailers had been a sort of tripodic ectoplasm.'

'That wasn't in System B303, though, was it?'

'Obviously not.' The old man came out in Swenson's snappishness. 'It was a couple of years ago. A couple of years ago System B303 was enjoying the doubtful benefits of proto-Elizabethan rule. As it still is.'

'Sorry. Stupid of me.'

'Some of you young men,' said Swenson, going over to the bank of monitor screens, 'expect too much of Time. You expect historical Time to be as plastic as the other kinds. Because the microchronic and macrochronic flows can be played with, you consider we ought to be able to do the same thing with – '

'Sorry, sorry, *sorry*. I just wasn't thinking.' With so much else on his mind, was it surprising that he should be temporarily ungeared to the dull realities of clockwork time, solar time?

'That's the trouble with you young – Ah,' said Swenson with satisfaction, 'that was a beautiful changeover.' With the smoothness of the tongue gliding from one phonemic area to another, the temporal path had become a spatial one. The uncountable megamiles between Earth and System B303 had been no more to their ship than, say, a two-way transatlantic flipover. And now, in reach of this other Earth – so dizzyingly far away that it was the same as their own, though at an earlier stage of their own Earth's history – the substance vedmum had slid them, as from one dream to another, into a world where solid objects might subsist, so alien as to be familiar, fulfilling the bow-bent laws of the cosmos. Swenson, who had been brought up on the interchangeability of time and space, could yet never cease to marvel at the miracle of the almost yawning casualness with which the *nacheinander* turned into the *nebeneinander* (there was no doubt, the old German words caught it best!). So far the monitor screens showed nothing, but tape began to whir out from the crystalline corignon machine in the

8

dead centre of the control turret — cold and accurate information about the solar system they were now entering. Swenson read it off, nodding, a Nordic spruce of a man glimmering with chemical youth. Paley looked at him, leaning against the bulkhead, envying the tallness, the knotty strength. But, he thought, Swenson could never disguise himself as an inhabitant of a less well-nourished era. He, Paley, small and dark as those far-distant Silurians of the dawn of Britain, could creep into the proto-Elizabethan England they would soon be approaching and never be noticed as an alien.

'Amazing how insignificant the variants are,' said Swenson. 'How finite the cosmos is, how shamefully incapable of formal renewals — '

'Oh, come,' smiled Paley.

'When you consider what the old musicians could do with a mere twelve notes — '

'The human mind,' said Paley, 'can travel in a straight line. The cosmos is curved.'

Swenson turned away from the billowing mounds of tape, saw that the five-manual console was flicking lights smoothly and happily, then went over to an instrument panel whose levers called for muscle, for the blacksmith rather than the organist. 'Starboard,' he said. '15.8. Now we play with gravities.' He pulled hard. The monitor screen showed band after band of light, moving steadily upwards. 'This, I think, should be — ' He twirled a couple of corrective dials on a shoulder-high panel above the levers. 'Now,' he said. 'Free fall.'

'So,' said Paley, 'we're being pulled by — '

'Exactly.' And then, 'You're quite sure you want to go through with this?'

'You know as well as I do,' smiled Paley patiently, 'that I *have* to go through with it. For the sake of scholarship. For the sake of my reputation.'

'Reputation,' snorted Swenson. Then, looking towards the monitors, he said, 'Ah. Something coming through.'

Mist, swirling cloud, a solid shape peeping intermittently out of vapour porridge. Paley came over to look. 'It's the Earth,' he said in wonder.

'It's *their* Earth.'

'The same as ours. America, Africa – '

'The configuration's slightly different, see, down there at the southern tip of – '

'Madagascar's a good deal smaller.'

'The cloud's come over again.' Paley looked and looked. It was unbelievable.

'Think,' said Swenson kindly, 'how many absolutely incomputable systems there have to be before you can see the pattern of creation starting all over again. This seems wonderful to you because you just can't conceive how many myriads upon myriads of other worlds are *not* like our own.'

'And the stars,' said Paley, a thought striking him; 'I mean, the stars they can actually see from there, from their London, say – are they the same stars as ours?'

Swenson shrugged at that. 'Roughly,' he said. 'There's a rough kinship. But,' he explained, 'we don't properly know yet. Yours is only the tenth or eleventh trip, remember. To be exact about it all, you're the first to go to B303 England. What is it, when all's said and done, but the past? Why go to the past when you can go to the future?' His nostrils widened with complacency. 'G9,' he said. 'I've done that trip a few times. It's pleasant to know one can look forward to another twenty years of life. I saw it there, quite clearly, a little plaque in Rostron Place: *To the memory of G. F. Swenson, 1963–2084.*'

'We have to check up on history,' said Paley, mumbling a little. His own quest seemed piddling: all this machinery, all this expertise in the service of a rather mean inquiry. 'I have to know whether William Shakespeare really wrote those plays.'

Swenson, as Paley expected, snorted. 'A nice sort of thing to want to find out,' he said. 'He's been dead just five hundred years this year, and you want to prove that there's nothing to celebrate. Not,' he added, 'that that sort of thing's much in my line. I've never had much time for poetry. Aaaaah.' He interposed his own head between Paley's and the screen, peering. The pages of the atlas had been turned; now Europe alone swam towards them. 'Now,' said Swenson, 'I must set the exactest course of all.' He worked at dials, frowning but humming happily, then beetled at Paley, saying: 'Oughtn't you to be getting ready?'

Paley blushed that, with a huge swath of the cosmos spent in near-idleness, he should have to rush things as they approached their port. He took off his single boiler-suit of a garment and drew from the locker his Elizabethan fancy-dress. Shirt, trunks, codpiece, doublet, feathered French hat, slashed shoes – clothes of synthetic cloth that was an exact simulacrum of old-time weaving, the shoes of good leather hand-made. And then there was the scrip with its false bottom; hidden therein was a tiny two-way signaller. Not that, if he got into difficulties, it would be of much use: Swenson was (and these were strict orders) to come back for him in a year's time. The signaller was to show where he was and that he was still there, a guest of the past, really a stowaway. Swenson had to move on yet farther into space; Professor Shimmins to be picked up in FH78, Dr Guan Moh Chan in G210, Paley collected on the way back. Paley tested the signaller, then checked the open and honest contents of his scrip: chief among these was a collection of the works of William Shakespeare – not the early works, though: only six of the works which, in this B303 year of A.D. 1595, had not yet been written. The plays had been copied from a facsimile of the First Folio in fairly accurate Elizabethan script; the paper too was a goodish imitation of the tough coarse stuff that Elizabethan drama-tists wrote on. For the rest, Paley had powdered prophylac-tics in little bags and, most important of all, gold – angels fire-new, the odd portague, dollars.

'Well,' said Swenson, with the faintest twinge of excite-ment, 'England, here we come.' Paley looked down on familiar river-shapes – Tees, Humber, Thames. He gulped, running through his drill swiftly. 'Count-down starts now,' said Swenson. A synthetic voice in the port bulkhead began ticking off cold seconds from 300. 'I'd better say good-bye then,' gulped Paley, opening the trap in the deck which led to the tiny jet-powered very-much-one-man aircraft. 'You should come down in the Thames estuary,' said Swenson. '*Au revoir*, not good-bye. I hope you prove whatever it is you want to prove.' 200 – 199 – 198. Paley went down, settled himself in the seat, checked the simple controls. Waiting took, it seemed, an age. He smiled wryly, seeing himself, an Elizabethan, with his hands on the wheel of a twenty-first century miniature jet aircraft. 60 – 59 – 58. He checked his Elizabethan vowels. He went over his fictitious provenance: a young man from Norwich with stage ambitions ('See, here have I writ a play and a goodly one'). The synthetic voice, booming here in the small cabin, counted to its limit. 4 – 3 – 2 – 1.

Zero. Paley zeroed out of the belly of the mother-ship, suddenly calm, then elated. It was moonlight, the green countryside slept. The river was a glory of silver. His course had been pre-set by Swenson; the control available to him was limited, but he came down smoothly on the water. What he had to do now was to ease himself to the shore. The little motor purred gently as he steered in moonlight. The river was broad here, so that he seemed to be in a world all water and sky. The shore neared – it was all trees, sedge, thicket; there was no sign of habitation, not even of another craft. What would another craft have thought, sighting him? He had no fears about that: with its wings folded, the little air-boat looked, from a distance, like some nondescript barge, so well had it been camouflaged. And now, to be safe, he had to hide it, cover it with greenery in the sedge. But, first, before disembarking, he must set the time-switch that would, when he was safe ashore, render the metal of the fuselage high-charged, lethally repellent of all would-be boarders. It was a pity, but there it was. It would automatically switch off in a year's time, in twelve months to a day. In the meantime, what myths, what madness would the curious examiner, the chance finder generate, tales uncredited by sophisticated London?

And now, London, here he came.

Paley, launched on his night's walk up-river, found the going easy enough. The moon lighted field-paths, stiles. Here and there a small farmhouse slept. Once he thought he heard a distant whistled tune. Once he thought he heard a town clock strike. He had no idea of the month or day or time of night, but he guessed that it was late spring and some three hours or so off dawn. The year 1595 was certain, according to Swenson. Time functioned here as on true Earth, and two years before Swenson had taken a man to Muscovy, where they computed according to the Christian system, and the year had been 1593. Paley, walking, found the air gave good rich breathing, but from time to time he was made uneasy by the unfamiliar configurations of the stars. There was Cassiopeia's Chair, Shakespeare's first name's drunken initial, but there were constellations he had not seen before. Could the stars, as the Elizabethans themselves believed, modify history? Could this Elizabethan London, because it looked up at stars unknown on true Earth, be identical with that other one that was only now known from books? Well, he would soon know.

London did not burst upon him, a monster of grey stone. It came upon him gradually and gently, houses set in fields and amid trees, the cool suburbs of the wealthy. And then, like a muffled trumpet under the sinking moon, the Tower. And then came the crammed houses, all sleeping. Paley breathed in the smell of this summer London, and he did not like what he smelled. It was a complex of old rags and fat and dirt, but it was also a smell he knew from the time he had flipped over to Borneo and timidly penetrated the periphery of the jungle: it was, somehow, a jungle smell.

And, as if to corroborate this, a howl arose in the distance, but it was a dog's howl. Dogs, man's best friend, here in outer space; dog howling to dog across the inconceivable vastness of the cosmos. And then came a human voice and the sound of boots on the cobbles. 'Four of the clock and a fine morning.' He instinctively flattened himself in an alley-way, crucified against the dampish wall. The time for his disclosure was not quite yet. He tasted the vowel-sounds of the bellman's call – nearer to American than to present-day British English. 'Fowrrr "vth" cluck.' And then, at last knowing the time and automatically feeling for a stopped wrist-watch that was not there, he wondered what he should do till day started. Here were no hotels with clerks on all-night duty. He tugged at his dark beard (a three months' growth) and then decided that, as the sooner he started on his scholar's quest the better, he would walk to Shoreditch where the Theatre was. Outside the City's boundaries, where the play-hating City Council could not reach, it was, history said, a new and handsome structure. A scholar's zest, the itch to see, came over him and made him forget the cool morning wind that was rising. His knowledge of the London of his own century gave him little help by way of street-orientation. He walked north – the Minories, Houndsditch, Bishopsgate – and, as he walked, he retched once or twice involuntarily at the stench from the kennel. There was a bigger, richer, filthier, obscener smell beyond this, and this he thought must come from Fleet Ditch. He dug into his scrip and produced a pinch of powder; this he placed on his tongue to quieten his stomach.

Not a mouse stirring as he walked, and there, under rolling cloud all besilvered, he saw it, he saw it, the Theatre, with something like disappointment. It was mean wood rising above wooden paling, its roof shaggily thatched. Things were always smaller than one expected, always more ordinary. He wondered if it might be possible to go in. There seemed to be no night-watchman protecting it. Before approaching the entrance (a door for an outside privy rather than a gate to the temple of the Muses) he took in the whole moonlit scene, the mean houses, the cobbles, the astonishing and unexpected greenery all about. And then he saw his first living animals.

Not a mouse stirring, had he thought? But those creatures with long tails were surely rats, a trio of them nibbling at some dump of rubbish not far from the way in to the Theatre. He went warily nearer, and the rats at once scampered off, each filament of whisker clear in the light. They were rats as he knew rats – though he had only seen them in the laboratories of his university – with mean bright eyes and thick meaty tails. But then he saw what they had been eating.

Dragged out from the mound of trash was a human fore-arm. In some ways Paley was not unprepared for this. He had soaked in images of traitor heads stuck on Temple Bar, bodies washed by three tides and left to rot on Thames shore, limbs hacked off at Tyburn (Marble Arch in his day) and carelessly left for the scavengers. (Kites, of course, kites. Now the kites would all be roosting.) Clinically, his stomach calm from the medicine he had taken, he examined the gnawed raw thing. There was not much flesh off it yet: the feast had been interrupted at its beginning. On the wrist, though, was a torn and pulpy patch which made Paley frown – something anatomically familiar but, surely, not referrable to a normal human arm. It occurred to him for just a second that this was rather like an eye-socket, the eye wrenched out but the soft bed left, still not completely ravaged. And then he smiled that away, though it was difficult to smile.

He turned his back on the poor human relic and made straight for the entrance-door. To his surprise it was not locked. It creaked as he opened it, a sort of voice of welcome to this world of 1595 and its strange familiarity. There it was – tamped earth for the groundlings to tamp down yet further; the side-boxes; the jutting apron-stage; the study uncurtained; the tarrass; the tower with its flagstaff. He breathed deeply, reverently. This was the Theatre. And then –

'Arrr, catched ye at it!' Paley's heart seemed about to leap from his mouth like a badly fitting denture. He turned to meet his first Elizabethan. Thank God, he looked normal enough, though filthy. He was in clumsy boots, goose-turd-coloured hose, and a rancid jerkin. He tottered a little as though drunk, and, as he came closer to peer into Paley's face, Paley caught a frightful blast of ale-breath. The man's eyes were glazed and he sniffed deeply and long at Paley as though trying to place him by scent. Intoxicated, unfocused, thought Paley with contempt, and as for having the nerve to sniff.... Paley spoke up, watching his vowels with care:

'I am a gentleman from Norwich, but newly arrived. Stand some way off, fellow. Know you not your betters when you see them?'

'I know not thee, nor why tha should be here at dead of night.' But he stood away. Paley glowed with small triumph, the triumph of one who has, say, spoken home-learnt Russian for the first time in Moscow and has found himself perfectly understood. He said:

'Thee? *Thee?* I will not be thee-and-thou'd so, fellow. I would speak with Master Burbage.'

'Which Master Burbage, the young or the old?'

'Either. I have writ plays and fain would show them.'

The watchman, as he must evidently be, sniffed at Paley again. 'Gentleman you may be, but you smell not like a Christian. Nor do you keep Christian hours.'

'As I say, I am but newly arrived.'

'I see not your horse. Nor your traveller's cloak.'

'They are – I have left them at mine inn.'

The watchman muttered. 'And yet you say you are but newly arrived. Go to.' Then he chuckled and, at the same time, delicately advanced his right hand towards Paley as though about to bless him. 'I know what 'tis,' he said, chuckling. ''Tis some naughty meeting, th'hast trysted ringading with some wench, nay, some wife rather, nor has she belled out the morn.' Paley could make little of this. 'Come,' said the man, 'chill make for 'ee an th' hast the needful.' Paley looked blank. 'An tha wants bedding,' the man said more loudly. Paley caught that, he caught also the significance of the open palm and wiggling fingers. Gold. He felt in his scrip and produced an angel. The man's jaw dropped as he took it. 'Sir,' he said, hat-touching.

'Truth to tell,' said Paley, 'I am shut out of mine inn, late-returning from a visit and not able to make mine host hear with e'en the loudest knocking.'

'Arrrr,' and the watchman put his finger by his nose, a homely Earthly gesture, then scratched his cheek with the angel, finally, before stowing it in a little purse on his girdle, passing it a few times in front of his chest. 'With me, sir, come.'

He waddled speedily out, Paley following him with fast-beating pulse. 'Where go we, then?' he asked. He received no answer. The moon was almost down and there were the first intimations of summer dawn. Paley shivered in the wind; he wished he had brought a cloak with him instead of the mere intention of buying one here. If it was really a bed he was being taken to, he was glad. An hour or so's sleep in the warmth of blankets and never mind whether or not there would be fleas. On the streets nobody was astir, though Paley thought he heard a distant cat's concert – a painful courtship and even more painful copulation to follow, just as on real Earth. Paley followed the watchman down a narrow lane off Bishopsgate, dark and stinking. The effects of the medicine had worn off; he felt his gorge rise as before. But the stink, his nose noticed, was subtly different from before: it was, he thought in a kind of small madness, somehow swirling, redistributing its elements as though capable of autonomous action. He didn't like this one little bit. Looking up at the paling stars he felt sure that they too had done a sly job of refiguration, forming fresh constellations like a sand tray on top of a thumped piano.

'Here 'tis,' said the watchman, arriving at a door and knocking without further ado. 'Croshabels,' he winked. But the eyelid winked on nothing but glazed emptiness. He knocked again, and Paley said:

''Tis no matter. It is late, or early, to drag folk from their beds.' A young cock crowed near, brokenly, a prentice cock.

'Never one nor t'other. 'Tis in the way of a body's trade, aye.' Before he could knock again, the door opened. A cross and sleepy-looking woman appeared. She wore a filthy nightgown and, from its bosom, what seemed like an arum lily peered out. She thrust it back in irritably. She was an old Elizabethan woman, about thirty-eight, grey-haired. She cried:

'Ah?'

'One for one. A gentleman, he saith.' He took his angel from his purse and held it up. She raised a candle the better to see. The arum lily peeped out again. All smiles, she curtseyed Paley in. Paley said:

''Tis but a matter of a bed, madam.' The other two laughed at that 'madam'. 'A long and wearisome journey from Norwich,' he added. She gave a deeper curtsey, more mocking than before, and said, in a sort of croak:

'A bed it shall be and no pallet nor the floor neither. For the gentleman from Norwich where the cows eat porridge.' The watchman grinned. He was blind, Paley was sure he was blind; on his right thumb something seemed to wink richly. The door closed on him, and Paley and the madam were together in the rancid hallway.

'Follow follow,' she said, and she creaked first up the stairs. The shadows her candle cast were not deep; grey was filling the world from the east. On the wall of the stair-well were framed pictures. One was a crude woodcut showing a martyr hanging from a tree, a fire burning under him. Out of the smiling mouth words ballooned: AND YETTE I SAYE THAT MOGRADON GIUETH LYFE. Another picture showed a king with crown, orb, sceptre and a third eye set in his forehead. 'What king is that?' asked Paley. She turned to look at him in some amazement. 'Ye know naught in Norwich,' she said, 'God rest ye and keep ye all.' Paley asked no further questions and kept his wonder to himself at another picture they passed: 'Q. Horatius Flaccus' it said, but the portrait was of a bearded Arab. Was it not Averroes?

The madam knocked loudly on a door at the top of the stairs. 'Bess, Bess,' she cried. 'Here's gold, lass. A cleanly and a pretty man withal.' She turned to smile at Paley. 'Anon will she come. She must deck herself like a bride.' From the bosom of her nightgown the lily again poked out and Paley thought he saw a blinking eye enfolded in its head. He began to feel the tremors of a very special sort of fear, not a terror of the unknown so much as of the known. He had rendered his flying-boat invulnerable; this world could not touch it. Supposing it were possible that this world was in some manner rendered invulnerable by a different process. A voice in his head seemed to say, with great clarity: 'Not with impunity may one disturb the – ' And then the door opened and the girl called Bess appeared, smiling professionally. The madam said, smiling also:

'There then, as pretty a mutton-slice as was e'er sauced o'er.' And she held out her hand for money. Confused, Paley dipped into his scrip and pulled out a clanking dull-gleaming handful. He told one coin into her hand and she still waited. He told another, then another. She seemed satisfied, but Paley seemed to know that it was only a temporary satisfaction. 'We have wine,' she said. 'Shall I – ?' Paley thanked her: no wine. The grey hair on her head grew erect. She curtseyed off.

Paley followed Bess into the bedchamber, on his guard now. The ceiling beat like a pulse. 'Piggesnie,' croaked Bess, pulling her single garment down from her bosom. The breasts swung and the nipples ogled him. They were, as he had expected, eyes. He nodded in something like satisfaction. There was, of course, no question of going to bed now. 'Honeycake,' gurgled Bess, and the breast-eyes rolled, the long lashes swept up and down, up and down coquettishly. Paley clutched his scrip tightly to him. If this distortion—likely, as far as he could judge, to grow progressively worse — if this scrambling of sense-data were a regular barrier against intrusion, why was there not more information about it on Earth? Other time-travellers had ventured forth and come back unharmed and laden with sensible records. Wait, though: had they? How did one know? There was Swenson's mention of Wheeler, gaoled in the Middle Ages by chunks of tripodic ectoplasm. 'White-haired and gibbering when we got him aboard.' Swenson's own words. How about Swenson's own vision of the future — a plaque showing his own birth and death dates? Perhaps the future did not object to intrusion from the past. But (Paley shook his head as though he were drunk, beating back sense into it) it was not a question of past and future, it was a question of other worlds existing *now*. The now-past was completed, the now-future was completed. Perhaps that plaque in Rostron Place, Brighton, showing Swenson's death some twenty years off, perhaps that was an illusion, a device to engender satisfaction rather than fear but still to discourage interference with the pattern. 'My time is short,' Paley suddenly said, using urgent twenty-first century phonemes, not Elizabethan ones. 'I will give you gold if you will take me to the house of Master Shakespeare.'

'Maister – ?'

'Shairkspeyr.'

Bess, her ears growing larger, stared at Paley with a growing montage of film battle-scenes playing away on the wall behind her. 'Th'art not that kind. Women tha likes. That I see in thy face.'

'This is urgent. This is business. Quick. He lives, I think, in Bishopsgate.' He could find out something before the epistemological enemies took over. And then what? Try and live. Keep sane with signals in some quiet spot till a year was past. Signal Swenson, receive Swenson's reassurances in reply; perhaps – who knew? – hear from far time-space that he was to be taken home before the scheduled date, instructions from Earth, arrangements changed . . .

'Thou knowest,' said Paley, 'what man I mean. Master Shakespeare the player at the Theatre.'

'Aye aye.' The voice was thickening fast. Paley said to himself: It is up to me to take in what I wish to take in; this girl has no eyes on her breasts, that mouth forming under her chin is not really there. Thus checked, the hallucinations wobbled and were pushed back temporarily. But their strength was great. Bess pulled on a simple dress over her nakedness, took a worn cloak from a closet. 'Gorled maintwise,' she said. Paley pushed like mad, the words unscrambled. 'Give me money now,' she said. He gave her a portague.

They tiptoed downstairs. Paley tried to look steadily at the pictures in the stair-well, but there was no time to make them tell the truth. The stairs caught him off his guard and changed to an escalator of the twenty-first century. He whipped them back to trembling stairhood. Bess, he was sure, would melt into some monster capable of turning his heart to stone if he let her. Quick. He held the point-of-day in the sky by a great effort. There were a few people on the street. He durst not look on them. 'It is far?' he asked. Cocks crowed, many and near, mature cocks.

'Not far.' But nothing could be far from anything in this cramped and toppling London. Paley strained to keep his sanity. Sweat dripped from his forehead and a drop caught on the scrip which he hugged to himself like a stomach-ache. He examined it as he walked, stumbling often on the cobbles. A drop of salty water from his pores. Was it of this alien world or of his own? If he cut off his hair and left it lying, if he dunged in that foul jakes there, from which a three-headed woman now appeared, would this B303 London reject it, as a human body will reject a grafted kidney? Was it perhaps not a matter of natural law but of some God of the system, a God against Whom, the devil on one's side, one could prevail? Was it God's club-rules he was pushing against, not some deeper inbuilt necessity? Anyway, he pushed, and Elizabethan London, in its silver dawn, steadied, rocked, steadied, held. But the strain was terrific.

'Here, sir.' She had brought him to a mean door which warned Paley that it was going to turn into water and flow down the cobbles did he not hold its form fast. 'Money,' she said. But Paley had given enough. He scowled and shook his head. She held out a fist which turned into a winking bearded man's face, threatening. He raised his own hand, flat, to slap her. She ran off, whimpering, and he turned the raised hand to a fist that knocked. His knock was slow in being answered. He wondered how much longer he could maintain this desperate holding of the world in position. If he slept, what would happen? Would it all dissolve and leave him howling in cold space when he awoke?

'Aye, what is't, then?' It was a misshapen ugly man with a row of bright blinking eyes across his chest, a chest left bare by his buttonless shirt. It was not, it could not be, William Shakespeare. Paley said, wondering at his own ability to enunciate the sounds with such exact care:

'Oi ud see Maister Shairkespeyr.' He was surlily shown in, a shoulder-thrust indicating which door he must knock at. This, then, was *it*. Paley's heart martelled desperately against his breastbone. He knocked. The door was firm oak, threatening no liquefaction.

'Aye?' A light voice, a pleasant voice, no early morning crossness in it. Paley gulped and opened the door and went in. Bewildered, he looked about him. A bedchamber, the clothes on the bed in disorder, a table with papers on it, a chair, morning light framed by the tight-shut window. He went over to the papers; he read the top sheet ('. . . giue it to him lest he raise all hell again with his fractuousness'), wondering if there was perhaps a room adjoining whence came that voice. Then he heard the voice again, behind him:

''Tis not seemly to read a gentleman's private papers lacking his permission.' Paley spun about to see, dancing in the air, a reproduction of the Droeshout portrait of Shakespeare, square in a frame, the lips moving but the eyes unanimated. He tried to call but could not. The talking woodcut advanced on him – 'Rude, mannerless, or art thou some Privy Council spy?' – and then the straight sides of the frame bulged and bulged, the woodcut features dissolved, and a circle of black lines and spaces tried to grow into a solid body. Paley could do nothing; his paralysis would not even permit him to shut his eyes. The solid body became an animal shape, indescribably gross and ugly – some spiked sea-urchin, very large, nodding and smiling with horrible intelligence. Paley forced it into becoming a more nearly human shape. His heart sank in depression totally untinged by fear to see standing before him a fictional character called 'William Shakespeare', an actor acting the part. Why could he not get in touch with the *Ding an sich*, the Kantian noumenon? But that was the trouble – the thing-in-itself was changed by the observer into whatever phenomenon the categories of time-space-sense imposed. He took courage and said:

'What plays have you writ to date?'

Shakespeare looked surprised. 'Who asks this?'

Paley said, 'What I say you will hardly believe. I come from another world that knows and reveres the name of Shakespeare. I believe that there was, or is, an actor named William Shakespeare. That Shakespeare wrote the plays that carry his name – this I will not believe.'

'So,' said Shakespeare, tending to melt into a blob of tallow badly sculpted into the likeness of Shakespeare, 'we are both to be unbelievers, then. For my part, I will believe anything. You will be a sort of ghost from this other world you speak of. By rights, you should have dissolved at cockcrow.'

'My time may be as short as a ghost's. What plays do you claim to have written up to this moment?' Paley spoke the English of his own day. Though the figure before him shifted and softened, tugging towards other shapes, the

eyes changed little, shrewd and intelligent eyes, modern.
And now the voice said:

'Claim? *Heliogabalus, A Word to Fright a Whoremaster,
The Sad Reign of Harold First and Last, The Devil in Dulwich.* . . .
Oh, many and many more.'

'Please.' Paley was distressed. Was this truth or teasing,
truth or teasing of this man or of his own mind, a mind
desperate to control the *données*, the sense-data, make them
make sense? On the table there, the mass of papers. 'Show
me,' he said. 'Show me somewhat,' he pleaded.

'Show me your credentials,' said Shakespeare, 'if we are
to talk of showing. Nay,' and he advanced merrily towards
Paley, 'I will see for myself.' The eyes were very bright now
and shot with oddly sinister flecks. 'A pretty boy,' said
Shakespeare. 'Not so pretty as some, as one, I would say,
but apt for a brief tumble of a summer's morning before the
day warms.'

'Nay,' said Paley, 'nay,' backing and feeling that
archaism to be strangely frivolous, 'touch me not.' The ad-
vancing figure became horribly ugly, the neck swelled, eyes
glinted on the backs of the approaching hands. The face
grew an elephantine proboscis, wreathing, feeling; two or
three suckers sprouted from its end and blindly waved towards Paley. Paley dropped his scrip the better to struggle.
The words of this monster were thick, they turned into
grunts and lallings. Pushed into the corner by the table,
Paley saw a sheet of paper much blotted ('Never blotted a
line,' did they say?):

> I haue bin struggling striuing? seeking? how I
>   may compair
> This jailhouse prison? where I liue unto the
>   earth world
> And that and for because

The scholar was still there, the questing spirit clear while the
body fought to keep off those huge hands, each ten-fingered.
The scholar cried:

'*Richard II!* You are writing *Richard II?*'

It seemed to him, literature's Claude Bernard, that he should risk all to get that message through to Swenson, that *Richard II* was, in 1595, being written by Shakespeare. He suddenly dipped to the floor, grabbed his scrip and began to tap through the lining at the key of the transmitter. Shakespeare seemed taken by surprise by this sudden cessation of resistance; he put out forks of hands that grasped nothing. Paley, blind with sweat, panting hard, tapped: 'R2 by ws.' Then the door opened.

'I did hear noise.' It was the misshapen ugly man with eyes across his bare chest, uglier now, his shape changing constantly though abruptly, as though set on by silent and invisible hammers. 'He did come to attack tha?'

'Not for money, Tomkin. He hath gold enow of's own. See.' The scrip, set down before so hurriedly, had spilt out its gold on the floor. Paley had not noticed; he should have transferred that gold to his –

'Aye, gold.' The creature called Tomkin gazed on it greedily. 'The others that came so brought not gold.'

'Take the gold and him,' said Shakespeare carelessly. 'Do what you will with both.' Tomkin oozed towards Paley. Paley screamed, attacking feebly with the hand that held the scrip. Tomkin's claw snatched it without trouble.

'There's more within,' he drooled.

'Did I not say thou wouldst do well in my service?' said Shakespeare.

'And here is papers.'

'Ah, papers.' And Shakespeare took them. 'Carry him to the Queen's Marshal. The stranger within our gates. He talks foolishly, like the Aleman that came before. Wildly, I would say. Of other worlds, like a madman. The Marshal will know what to do.'

'But,' screamed Paley, grabbed by strong shovels of hands, 'I am a gentleman. I am from Norwich. I am a playwright, like yourself. See, you hold what I have written.'

'First a ghost, now from Norwich,' smiled Shakespeare,

hovering in the air like his portrait again, a portrait holding papers. 'Go to. Are there not other worlds, like unto our own, that sorcery can make men leave to visit this? I have heard such stories before. There was a German –'

'It's true, true, I tell you.' Paley clung to that, clinging also to the chamber door with his nails, the while Tomkin pulled at him.

'You are the most intelligent man of these times! You can conceive of it!'

'And of poets yet unborn also? Drythen, or some such name, and Lord Tennis-balls, and a drunken Welshman and P. S. Eliot? You will be taken care of like that other.'

'But it's true, true!'

'Come your ways,' growled Tomkin. 'You are a Bedlam natural.' And he dragged Paley out, Paley collapsing, frothing, raving. Paley raved: 'You're not real any of you. It's you who are the ghosts! *I'm* real, it's all a mistake, let me go, let me explain!'

'Tis strange he talks,' growled Tomkin. And he dragged him out.

'Shut the door' said Shakespeare. Tomkin kicked it shut. The screaming voice went, over thumping feet, down the passage-way without. Soon it was quiet enough to sit and read.

These were, thought Shakespeare, good plays. Strange that one of them was about, as far as he could judge, a usurious Jew. This Norwich man had evidently read Marlowe and seen the dramatic possibilities of an evil Lopez-type character. Shakespeare had toyed with the idea of a play like this himself. And here it was, ready done for him. And there were a couple of promising looking histories here, too, about King Henry IV. And here a comedy called *Much Ado About Nothing*. Gifts, godsends! He smiled. He remembered that Aleman, Doctor Schleyer or some such name, who had come with a story like this madman (mad? Could madmen do work like this? 'The lunatic, the lover and the poet': a good line in that play about fairies Schleyer had brought. Poor Schleyer had died of the plague). Those plays Schleyer had brought had been good plays, but not, perhaps, quite so good as these.

Shakespeare furtively (though he was alone) crossed himself. When poets had talked of the Muse had they perhaps meant visitants like this, now screaming feebly in the street, and the German Schleyer and that one who swore, under torture, that he was from Virginia in America, and that in America they had universities as good as Oxford or Leyden or Wittenburg, nay better? Well whoever they were, they were heartily welcome so long as they brought plays. That Richard II of Schleyer's was, perhaps, in need of the emendations he was now engaged on, but the earlier work, from Henry VI on, had been popular. He read the top sheet of this new batch, stroking his auburn beard silvered, a fine grey eye reading. He sighed and before crumpling a sheet of his own work on the table, he read it. Not good, it limped, there was too much magic in it. Ingenio the Duke said:

> Consider gentlemen as in the sea
> All earthly life finds like and parallel
> So in far distant skies our lives be aped
> Each hath a twin, each action hath a twin,
> And twins have twins galore and infinite
> And e'en these stars be twinn'd....

Too fantastic, it would not do. He threw it into the rubbish box which Tomkin would later empty. He took a clean sheet and began to copy in a fair hand:

The Merchant of Venice

Then on he went, not blotting a line.

Susan Hill

In the
Conservatory

From the beginning, theirs was a very public love affair. That is, they conducted it mainly in public places, and that out of choice, rather than of necessity. They both had a certain amount of time and money to spend on the relationship, so that it might have been nurtured in the quietness and privacy of town and country hotels, perhaps even of a flat. But they met in public, wanting somehow to prove the reality of it to themselves, by seeing and being seen.

It began at the party to celebrate the opening of Nancy's bookshop, in one of the Dickensian alleyways off Chancery Lane. *He* knew Nancy quite well, because he had been prevailed upon to help her select the stock, though he had had misgivings, it was not his field. He sold only – and sold very successfully – antiquarian books.

She scarcely knew Nancy at all, she had gone to the party in place of her husband, Boris, to whom the invitation was addressed. Boris never went to parties of any kind, but that did not stop the invitations coming. And she had gone with this purpose in mind – to meet someone. For she had decided some weeks beforehand that it ought to be her next experience. I am thirty-two years old, she told herself, eight years married and childless, what else is there for me? I am not unattractive, not unintelligent, yet I have never had any sort of an affair, before marriage or since, there is a whole world about which my friends talk and people write, and about which *I* know nothing. There are emotions, passions, jealousies and anxieties, which I do not understand. It is time, surely it is time . . .

Perhaps, after all, it was not as clear-cut, as fully conscious as that, perhaps there were many doubts and moments of disillusion. But the decision was in some sort made, and afterwards, she felt herself to be suddenly more vulnerable, more aware, she was receptive to glances and questions and implications. And then, it was only a question of time. Time, and the right choice.

She had arrived at Nancy's party, flushed and pretty with anticipation. Of course, Boris would never mind. Indeed, her dull certainty that Boris would not mind took a little of the edge off it all. Boris, preoccupied with his books on military history, Boris with his little leaden soldiers, drawn up in battalions all over the dining-table, Boris who was more of a stranger to her, now, than any of the people at Nancy's party – this was the Boris who would not mind.

And so, that was where they had met, one evening in Nancy's new shop, and then the following day, too, because *he* had half said, and *she* had half said, that they might be somewhere in the British Museum at some point tomorrow. She had rushed all about that great mausoleum, up and down marble staircases, until her legs ached, among all the Malay students and school parties from Lancashire, in and out of manuscript rooms and sculpture rooms and print rooms, galleries full of Egyptian mummies and Anglo-Saxon drinking vessels and oriental porcelain, and still she had not found him anywhere. Only later, after she had drunk a cup of grey coffee and slipped off her shoes under the table, and then gone wearily back, there he had been, looking at her behind one of the racks of postcards in the publications hall. His eyes were the colour of pebbles on a winter beach.

After that, for several weeks, they always met in the British Museum, a different room each day, she had never seen so much of it, never learned so much, by accident, in her life before. They moved on to the National Portrait

Gallery, then, and the Tate, and the Musical instruments rooms of the V and A, they sat on innumerable, leather-covered benches, and stood before important paintings and drank tea in the dreary tea-rooms, talked to one another, touched one another rather formally, explored the initial avenues of their affair.

Soon, they took to going farther afield, as though they now felt able to extend the boundaries of their relationship, to view it against a new background. He had to travel, in any case, buying his books, and she herself was a free agent, neither children or work claimed her, and Boris did not care. They took their time over finding country hotels, first of all for lunch or tea, but later, when the spring came, they began to sleep together. Sparingly, at first. In the mornings, she awoke and got out of bed to stare in the mirror at herself, expecting to see a change. Here I am, she said, and there he is and it must be that I am now truly living, that this is experience ...

It was at about this time, in their search for public places out of London, for castles and abbeys and country homes, that they came across Fewings. And Fewings seemed to them to be some kind of architectural terminus, a statement, in bricks and mortar, of all that they were experiencing in their affair. Once they had found Fewings, and the convenient Inn called the Four in Hand, in a village close by, they went nowhere else.

Fewings was the ugliest house either of them had ever seen, a Victorian Gothic fantasy, like one of mad Ludwig's Bavarian castles, all turrets and towers and crenellations of rose-pink brick. It *had* in fact been built, in the heart of the Kent countryside, by an Anglophile German count, who had seen it as his gift to England.

When he died, at the turn of the century, he had left Fewings, together with a wealthy trust for its upkeep, to the British nation. The nation, being obliged to accept it, had made a virtue out of necessity and erected signposts along all the main roads and posters in selected railway stations.

Paragraphs about Fewings appeared in local guide books, a caretaker was installed, gardeners and a curator were employed, and from March until October, the visitors came.

The grotesqueness of the house was more than matched by its bizarre contents, for the Count had been a collector. A whole wing, for instance, was given over to Chinoiserie, with life-size waxworks dressed as Mandarins and Cantonese executioners, lurking on the bends of stairs. In the cellars were instruments of torture, and, at the top of the building, galleries full of dolls, and miniature dolls' houses. There were the usual libraries full of morocco-bound books in glass cases, the usual guns and pistols and suits of armour, the usual oils and watercolours and prints – and other things besides, less usual and more alarming. There was something sinister about Fewings, the rooms had a certain smell. Very few people who came once ever wanted to return.

The gardens were rather a different matter, for the German Count had handed over the construction of them to an Englishman called Captain Smithers, who combined the enthusiasms of the amateur with the application and authority of a professional. He took twenty years to make, at Fewings, one of the great landscape gardens of England.

There was much topiary work, casting dark shadows of birds and lions couchant on to the sunlit grass, there were colonnades and formal terraces and large fountains, a Gothic arch of beeches and raised, circular lawns. It was a dramatic garden, devoid of prettiness except for one or two arbours hidden in the topiary here and there, overlooking the sunken flower beds. It was all rather severe, to complement the extravagances of the house, satisfying in its proportions yet wholly dramatic, a public garden, larger than any of the life that surrounding Kent might have to offer.

The drama of Fewings and its gardens was what appealed to them. That and its unexpectedness. For her part, too, she found it sinister, she had nightmares centred upon the place, and all of this contributed to her sense of heightened awareness, of real, true living. Each time they visited, they felt excitement, they discovered more and more rooms, new spiral staircases leading up into the towers and new corridors, ending in sudden window seats that gave startling views of the gardens below, and the rich countryside beyond. They experienced themselves through their experience of the house.

She liked to be frightened there, to have him leave her alone in the cellars, with all the black and grey steel instruments of torture and the cold whitewashed walls, the smell of dampness that came from being below the level of the earth. The long passages echoed to the ring of his footsteps, as he walked quickly away from her, and she was forced to run in terrified search of him, frantically going from room to room, getting lost and coming upon one of the costumed waxworks, before she did, at last, find him, and sobbed with relief. Fewings excited them, indeed, as nowhere else could have done. And afterwards, there was the small back bedroom at the Four in Hand.

But above all, she found herself drawn, in fear and fascination, to the conservatory that was built into the centre of the house like a great, covered court-yard, the glass roof ribbed and vaulted in the style of the Victorian railway stations. It had a wrought iron gallery running all the way around it, close to the sky. The German Count had spent most of his time here, in his last years, pacing around and around, wearing a long red dressing-gown. He had talked to himself all day and terrified the maids if they sought him out with news of a guest or a letter or a meal. As he walked, he had looked down upon the jungle he had made below.

He had imported every kind of tropical plant and creeper and now, years later, they crept up over the glass walls and then knitted together, to overhang the narrow pathways, trailing down their dark green leaves like great flat hands. The stems were thick as legs and arms, and all the time, one or other of the plants was throwing up gigantic flowers in vivid, unlikely colours, flame and scarlet, yellow and fuchsia pink, all striped and spotted and fantastically shaped. The conservatory was heated to a steaming temperature, by long, old-fashioned radiators hidden in the undergrowth, so that, however hard they cut everything back, it grew again twice as fast, the foliage and the flowers rampaged up and over the conservatory roof and the light that filtered through was a pale and curious green.

Down below, in the centre of it all, was the pond, thick with reeds and water-plants, below which slid the fish, slow, fat-bodied fish taken from the rivers of Central Africa and South America, dramatically coloured and marked. You could sit on the flat stone ledge that surrounded the pool, under the green umbrella of leaves, and smell the hot, sweet smell of the jungle. They came in here more and more, stayed for hours, shoulders and thighs touching, mesmerized by the stillness and the soft green light, saying nothing at all. Though once, at the very beginning, she had told him, 'This is the heart of the house, this is where we should always come,' and at once, she had felt foolish, for saying that had brought into the open some truth she did not wish to acknowledge, about the unreality, the *risibility* of their affair, and she had shrunk back at once. It does not do, she said, to analyse things, we should never make definitive statements about a relationship. She had read precisely that, somewhere recently.

To cover the moment's embarrassment, she had leaned forward and slid her hand into the warm, slightly glutinous water. It had come up against the body of a fish, and she cried out in horror, got up at once, pulling him after her, had made him take her away from the conservatory and from Fewings altogether. But before very long, she had to go back, she now seemed only able to savour their relationship to the full in the strange atmosphere of Fewings. She forced herself to sweat gently under the dark green canopy of leaves, watching the slow opening of an orange Hulura flower, pointed and starred and with purple stamens like long, furred tongues.

He, for his part, was not at all alarmed by the atmosphere at Fewings, it merely amused him, but he was excited by the effect it had upon her, it shocked him to see her violent delight and fear. He had always thought himself a dull man, leading a dull life, he had been too lethargic to seek out the experiences he thought he needed, if life were not entirely to pass him by, but he had so far had only the usual, the predictable relationships. She startled him profoundly, therefore, because she had sought him out, yet he had still not altogether shrugged off the lethargy, for he himself had done nothing, and he did nothing still. It was she who worked up their affair as she chose, and gave it its pattern and character; he watched and was manipulated by her and that seemed to be enough.

It was in the conservatory that she first caught sight of the boy, and was at once aware that she had, in fact, seen him several times before, about the house – disappearing ahead of them up some staircase, or standing in the corners of rooms, half hidden by the furniture. Until now, he had not registered himself upon her consciousness, and so she had paid no attention to him. Now, here he was, in the conservatory, looking at them between the thick, fleshy leaves, and yet not looking, his eyes focused elsewhere, or focused upon nothing at all. She moved suddenly, but he did not start. He stayed where he was, for several moments, and then turned and went slowly away with a curious, shuffling walk. A door scraped shut behind him, the sound muffled by the undergrowth.

One of the violently coloured tropical birds that lived up near the roof of the conservatory, flapped down, in a rush of wings and darting, turquoise blue tail.

'I want to go,' she said, pulling him to his feet, 'Now, quickly.'

The next time they came to Fewings, they saw the boy again.

In the Conservatory

The Musrys had come as caretakers to Fewings as soon as everything got under way again, after the war. Arthur wasn't well, his leg would never get properly better, they said, and it had seemed too good an opportunity to miss, with living in the country and a self-contained flat, and so forth. You thought twice about turning down jobs with self-contained flats, in those days. So they had come, though she had not been at all sure, not really, and the moment they had started to open up all the rooms, and get the stuff out of store, she knew why.

'It's a very funny place,' she had said, 'a very funny place indeed.' But that was all, because Arthur seemed keen, it had taken his fancy, and he didn't think so much about his leg and feel sorry for himself. So she kept her real feelings to herself, and made the most of the self-contained flat, tucked away in the East wing, not venturing farther than she must, into the rest of the house. In time, she had an army of morning cleaners, who came in a coach from the town, nine miles away, and she was in her element then, organizing them. They could always be sent into those parts of the house she didn't much care for.

So they had been here twenty-four years, and the boy Leonard for thirteen of them.

It was her younger sister's boy, and she had known about him right from the beginning, from the very first day that Amy was sick. It was what they had all expected of Amy sooner or later, but they hadn't expected her to die, nor that their mother would die, six days after. Amy had been going to live on at home, with her mother and the child, it was all arranged. Nobody knew anything at all about the child's father.

They were the only ones left, and so they had taken him themselves, and, although neither of them knew anything about children, they fitted their lives around him without any difficulty, because he was a good boy, he had not been a moment's trouble.

They didn't exactly know what was wrong with him, just

that, as it were, something was not quite right. He was very slow. He picked up his fork and spoon slowly and it was hard for him to grip things, or to separate his toys into piles, or judge how many stairs he had to clamber down, so that at first he was forever falling. He was nine before he was sure which shoe to put on which foot, and even now, they had trouble over laces.

But he was a very gentle child, he touched people and objects with the same soft, delicate touch, and he smiled a good deal, at almost anything. He loved Fewings. He went everywhere about the place with his father from being a tiny baby – because they called themselves mother and father to him and never told him the truth: where was the point? He would only be upset and never properly understand. They carried him about, and he was left in the window seats, or the carved oak settle, and he would wait, looking about him, quite content. He was very late in walking, almost three before he could climb the stairs, but after that, he was always going off into the house, they never knew exactly where. And because he was such an obedient child and would never touch anything after they had told him once that he was not to, they let him go, by himself, wherever he pleased. She was worried for a long time about the cellars, there were so many terrible things on which he could have accidents but his father told him that he could only walk about down there and never touch anything. He never touched.

Some things, of course, he *was* allowed to touch, mostly in winter, when there were no visitors and the curator only came once a month. They let him take the dolls and hold them, and when the guns were being cleaned, his father would balance one upon his outstretched hands. But not the books, for he had once let a book slip off his knees, and grabbed it back, in panic, by a single page, which tore. It was a big book of maps. He had sobbed for two hours, and on and off through the night, and for weeks afterwards, if he went by the doors of the library.

In the Conservatory

If they had been willing to send him away from them, he could have boarded in London at a special school, but they knew that Amy would not have let him go, and besides, what good would it do? To their own surprise, they found that they loved him, and so he went to the village school, where he learned what little he could, and was happy. At eleven, he had been taken by a school in the next town, and so, Arthur Musry had bought a motor bicycle and side-car and learned to drive it very cautiously, so that he could take the boy, and bring him back, each day. It was worst in winter, when his leg and the weather were bad.

They knew that he would always stay with them at Fewings, that he was never going to make his own way in the world, and they were only worried about how he might be if anything should happen to them. But he was happy enough, meanwhile, in the house and gardens after school and all through the holidays, doing little jobs, fetching and carrying. He knew every corner, every room and staircase and corridor, and he only wanted to be left to wander about, looking at everything, making sure that it was safe. He did not get in the way of the summer visitors, only watched them, fascinated, and sometimes, he would be able to direct them to this or that room, to the tea bar or the lavatories, and this delighted him, it made him feel necessary, though his speech was thick and slow, they could not always understand him. He never seemed to hold their subsequent impatience against them.

But it was the conservatory that he loved most of all. There were lizards hidden among the stones in the undergrowth, and small toads about the pond. He let them run over his hands, unafraid. Feeding the fish was the one job he had done quite by himself for some years, the keeper, who lived down in the village, had come to trust him over that. It was to the conservatory that the couple went first, if they wanted to find him.

He was there, just sitting, when they came upon him the

next time they visited Fewings. She had been saying something about Boris, and his floor-to-ceiling maps of German battlefields, laughing at the childishness of it, when they came around the path, towards the pond and saw him. She stopped dead.

'He's there,' she said, 'he's there again.' The boy took no notice of them, though she felt that he was aware, was listening.

'I keep on seeing him, now,' she said, 'why does he follow us?'

'Oh, surely he does not!' They always spoke half in whispers in the conservatory, there was something about the place that encouraged secrecy. 'I think he's just the care-taker's boy.'

'I don't like him, he watches us. I wish he would go away.'

They sat, some distance from him, under the leaves beside the pond. She laid each one of her fingers upon his. One of the birds began to chatter, Kuu-uup, Kuu-uup, Kuu-uup, in the branches above.

Later, they went up into the tower room at the remote, north end of the house, climbing up a dark staircase. They had found the bench seat, let into a narrow gap in the wall, quite by chance, and the tower housed only a few dull maps and suits of armour, nobody else bothered to come up here. The window looked directly down hundreds of giddy feet on to the top of the fountain. But this time, they arrived breathless, to find the boy already in the window-seat, staring down. She jumped back, giving a little cry of alarm, and then she was angry, for she felt spied upon, and the boy frightened her because there was something not right. This particular place was now quite spoiled for her. The boy got up and went at once, moving forward with his odd, slow walk, knees a little bent. He had still taken no notice of them. But she said in a hysterical voice, 'I don't like him, I wish we didn't have to keep seeing him here. He isn't quite right, he shouldn't be wandering about alone, I shall find somebody and complain.'

He calmed her eventually, and they forgot about the boy, they talked of themselves and their continuing amazement at the complexities of their affair. She was still absorbed in it, in the emotions she experienced and in the sense of acute awareness, of unreality. She had begun to keep a diary, for everything seemed too significant to lose. Now, when she read novels and saw plays, and talked to friends about such affairs, she understood everything exactly, it was all personally confirmed, and she felt herself to be part of the great, adult world of experience. For she said to him that she had never felt herself to be truly adult, until now.

Her one disappointment was that Boris did not care. She could not quite tell whether he knew about them or not, but whichever it was, she smarted under his indifference, and began to think of ways in which she might bring matters to a head with him, for surely the time had come for there to be some jealousy, some quarrels ending in tears and forgiveness. But Boris only marched his leaden soldiers up and down the dining-table, and smiled vaguely at a point beyond her shoulder, when she was going out. And did not care.

'You must see it,' she said, one afternoon in July, 'he *spies* upon us. If we manage to get away from the other visitors, we cannot get away from him. He is everywhere.'

'No, no, surely not. You've started to notice him, be irritated by him, that's all. I think perhaps he was always there.'

'No. He looks, he lies about in wait for us.'

That day, they had been walking through the Chinese rooms, and suddenly, he was there, sitting in a sedan chair, his eyes glistening, very still.

'He ought not to be *allowed* to,' she said, 'he will damage something.' And she had made a vague movement of her hands towards the boy, frowned very sternly, in order to shoo him away.

He laughed at her, the anger and discontent excited him. 'Poor child,' he said mildly, 'I'm sure he cannot help it,' and touched his hand to her bare arm, moving her away. They could have three nights, this time, in the bedroom at the Four in Hand, though he must spend some part of the days buying books at house sales.

But she could not stop thinking about the boy, even when they were away from Fewings. And while they were there, if she saw the back of him, disappearing along some corridor, or in the distance, pushing a barrow-load of grass cuttings across the lawn, the rest of their day was spoiled for her, she could not concentrate upon themselves.

While he went to one of his sales, therefore, she came alone, and looked about purposefully, for someone in charge.

'Surely it is not safe,' she said firmly, 'We have seen him poking about in this and that, sitting on the furniture, going up and down steep stairs. Surely he ought to be watched more carefully.'

Arthur Musry stared, reaching down to rub at the back of his bad leg. He didn't like her, had never liked her, and he had often wondered about them, always coming here, spending so much money on entrance tickets, wondered what they did all those afternoons, in the deserted rooms.

'Mightn't he hurt himself? How can he be safe, when he walks the way he does? He isn't the sort of boy who should have the run of a place like this, on his own.'

'He's all right,' Arthur Musry said, 'there's nothing wrong with him, he's a good boy. He'll not touch anything, not do anything. This is his home, isn't it? He's all right.'

'He *follows* us.' Her voice rose in desperation.

'Why should he do that?'

'*I* don't know why, I only know he does.'

He shook his head, and looked away from her, down the gravelled drive. If he could have been rid of her, turned her away the next time, he would have done so.

'He's all right,' he said again, sullen.

'I just don't like it when he watches us, and listens. When he follows.' She was almost in tears of rage, knowing there was nothing she could do, that she was in the wrong and the man could never be made to take her word, could never begin to understand.

'He was stupid,' she said later, in the bedroom, 'a stupid little man.'

The next time they went to Fewings, she caught hold of the boy in one of the dark passages and held his arm tightly, pushed her face into his and told him not to come near them, to go now, right away, to stop following and spying. He backed from her, eyes huge with alarm, and disappeared into the shadows, she heard his uncertain tread, fast as it could go, on the staircase. He had made straight for the conservatory, and that was where they too came, some time later, and found him hiding under the branches, with a small brown lizard resting on his hand.

He got up at once and backed away.

'That's all right,' she said, walking round and round the pond, trying to see down into the water, looking for the fish. 'He's gone, he won't do it again, that's all right.' And later, she said also, 'Poor child, he ought to be away some- where, he ought to be looked after. How can you blame him?' She sat down and began to talk to him about how she wanted to quarrel violently with Boris.

For three weeks, the boy would not go out of the flat, and at night he wet his bed and called out. They couldn't make sense of it, and got the doctor, who could find nothing wrong. He sat all day with a picture book or looking at the television, and he wanted to be near to them both, wherever they went, he went, and his shoes were suddenly on the wrong feet, he wore his jersey back to front until she noticed, and helped to dress him.

It was a long time before he would go back into the house alone. They had to coax him like a mouse out of a hole, his father had to keep calling to him, for reassurance. Gradually, he grew better, but his hands still trembled when he lifted anything, and he began to sleep-walk every night, they grew accustomed to lying tensely, listening for him.

During this time, Boris developed pleurisy, and she was preoccupied with her sense of guilt, and with her alarm at the idea that she would no longer want to continue with the affair, if Boris were to die.

But Boris did not die, he got better and went to convalesce in Ischia, and then they could visit Fewings again. She sat up in bed very early each morning to write a blue air-mail letter to her absent husband.

At Fewings, it was almost the end of the season. The lines of poplars were half-bare, half-brown, and Arthur Musry was out on the circular lawn with a besom, sweeping up leaves. 'We must go everywhere,' she said, her eyes very bright, '*every*where. This is the last time, there is such a lot to see and remember.' 'But it is only till March.' He laughed at her. 'There will be next year.' But she would not have him spoil her sense of occasion.

They left the conservatory until the very last.

The boy was better, much better, except that he still would not go up on to the landing where she had frightened him. He no longer wet the bed, or clutched at them suddenly, he ate his meals without making any mess. But something had happened, something was different, his mother knew that, and they had noticed it at school and wondered what had happened, and if he would improve. Arthur Musry remembered the woman, and said nothing.

For some time, he would not go into the conservatory either, but they talked to him about the fish, and asked didn't he want to feed them again? 'It's to build up his confidence,' his father said, 'we've got to do it, it's for the best. Let him get back to the fish and the animals, they'll help him, bring him round.'

In some way, they did, so that before very long he would venture in alone, as long as the door was left slightly open.

Shortly after this, he had a kind of fit, one of the cleaners found him just outside the library, his eyes rolled back into his head, legs twitching. He came round before the doctor arrived and seemed quite all right, was only a little pale, and confused over which hand ought to hold his fork. They gave him tablets and he went for a day to the hospital for tests, but nothing was told them, nothing was said.

She had been talking about the winter, and how different everything would be, for they would be meeting in London again and she wanted to start visiting his flat, because it happened to be quite close to the college at which Boris gave his military lectures. She foresaw new dangers in the continuation of their affair, she wanted to take risks and be in suspense, to be speculated over and talked about.

'Whatever you want,' he told her, laughing again, 'whatever you say.' For he saw how much even the anticipation of the winter was affecting her and knew that she would continue to act violently upon his emotions.

'Now,' she said, jumping up, '*now* the conservatory!'

She began to run down the staircases and along corridors, he panted and could scarcely keep up with her, the blood began to make a rushing sound in his ears.

The conservatory was very still, very quiet, the glass door slipped shut and she smelled the thick jungle smell and shivered a little, her skin shadowed green by the over-hanging branches.

They found the boy upside down in the pond, his head and shoulders underneath the flat water-plants, among the slow-moving fish, and only his legs sticking out over the side. She saw that the shoes were carefully fitted on to the wrong feet. The little canister of meal for the fish lay, overturned, on the floor.

He was making for the door to get help, he would have left her there, not thinking, if she had not stumbled out after him, making an odd, low noise in her throat and putting up her hands to her face. The glass door clicked gently shut, behind her.

They never came to Fewings again. She had known that they would not, even before it happened, known that events do not repeat themselves, and that by the end of the winter, she would have grown bored and started to look for something, someone, else, the next experience.

In the event, it could not go on even for as long as that, everything was changed, she surfaced like a diver into a grey and chilling world. For weeks, she could think of nothing but the boy, dead, among the fish, in the conservatory. They had to go to the near-by town, for the inquest, but she made him drive her straight back to London when it was over.

On his side, he sensed the change, saw that there was a deadness about her, and, knowing that it was at an end, was unexpectedly relieved. There was no final scene, no quarrel, no dramatic parting, as she had always anticipated. He gave her dinner that evening, and then drove her all the way home, got out of the car, and shook hands, strangely, on the doorstep. Once, a couple of months later, they did see one another in the Food Hall at Harrods, and he half-waved, she half-waved, hesitated, moved on. She bought veal and a whole Cheddar cheese, and when she got home with them, Boris had arranged his battalions of soldiers on the kitchen table, because there were workmen decorating the dining-room.

In the bathroom, she looked at her own face in the mirror and for the first time she saw a change.

Arthur Musry sold the motor bicycle and side-car, but that was all, they stayed on at Fewings because there was nowhere else for them to go, not after twenty four years, even if she did not really like it. Whenever he could, he avoided the conservatory. She resigned herself, said nothing, knowing that it would not be easy, these days, to find another job with a self-contained flat.

Susan Hill

How Soon Can I Leave?

The two ladies who lived together were called Miss Bartlett and Miss Roscommon.

Miss Roscommon, the older and stouter of the two, concealed her fear of life behind frank reference to babies and lavatories and the sexing of day-old chicks. It was well known that she had travelled widely as a girl, she told of her walking tours in Greece, and how she had driven an ambulance during the Spanish Civil War.

Miss Bartlett, who was only forty, cultivated shyness and self-effacement, out of which arose her way of leaving muttered sentences to trail off into the air, unfinished. Oh, do not take any notice of anything *I* may say, she meant, it is of no consequence, I am sorry to have spoken. . . . But the sentences drew attention to her, nevertheless.

'What was that?' people said, 'I beg your pardon, I didn't quite catch. . . . Do speak up. . . .' And so, she was forced to repeat herself and they, having brought it upon themselves, were forced to listen. She also protested helplessness in the face of everyday tools. It was Miss Roscommon who peeled all the potatoes and defrosted the refrigerator and opened the tins.

Their house, one of two white bungalows overlooking the bay, was called Tuscany.

When Miss Bartlett had finally come to live with Miss Roscommon, seven years before, each one believed that the step was taken for the good of the other. Miss Bartlett had been

47

living in one of the little stone cottages, opposite the harbour, working through the winter on the stock that she sold, from her front room and on a trestle outside, in summer. From November until March, there were no visitors to Mountsea. Winds and rain scoured the surface of the cliffs and only the lifeboat put out to sea. Miss Roscommon had taken to inviting Miss Bartlett up to the bungalow for meals.

'You should have a shop,' she had begun by saying, loading Miss Bartlett's plate with scones and home-made ginger jam, 'properly equipped and converted. It cannot be satisfactory having to display goods in your living-room. Why have you not thought of taking a shop?'

Miss Bartlett made marquetry pictures of the church, the lighthouse and the harbour, table-lamps out of lobster pots and rock worked over with shells. She also imported Italian straw baskets and did a little pewter work.

The idea of a shop had come to her, and been at once dismissed, in the first weeks after her coming to Mountsea. She was too timid to take any so definite a step, for, by establishing herself in a shop, with her name written up on a board outside, was she not establishing herself in the minds of others, as a shop*keeper*? As a girl, she had been impressed by her mother's constant references to her as dreamy and artistic, so that she could not possibly now see herself in the role of shopkeeper. Also, by having her name written up on that board, she felt that she would somehow be committing herself to Mountsea, and by doing that, finally abandoning all her hopes of a future in some other place. As a girl, she had looked out at the world, and seen a signpost, with arms pointing in numerous different directions, roads leading here, or here, or there. She had been quite unable to choose which road to take for, having once set out upon any of them, she would thereby be denying herself all the others. And what might I lose, she had thought, what opportunities shall I miss if I make the wrong choice?

So that, in the end, she had never chosen, only drifted through her life from this to that, waking every morning to the expectation of some momentous good fortune dropped in her lap.

'That cottage is damp,' said Miss Roscommon, allowing her persuasions to take on a more personal note, as they got to know one another better. 'I do not think you look after yourself properly. And a place of business should not have to double as a home.'

At first, Miss Bartlett shrank from the hints and persuasions, knowing herself to be easily swayed, fearful of being swept along on the tide of Miss Roscommon's decision. I am only forty years old, she said, there is plenty of opportunity left for me, I do not have to abandon hope by retreating into middle age, and life with another woman. Though certainly she enjoyed the meals the other cooked, the taste of home-baked pasties and stews and herb-flavoured vegetables.

'I'm afraid that I cannot cook,' she said, 'I live on milk and cheese and oven-baked potatoes. I would not know where to begin in the kitchen.' It did not occur to her that this was any cause for shame, and Miss Roscommon tut-tutted and floured the pastry-board, relieved to have, once again, a sense of purpose brought into her life.

'There were nine of us in the family,' she said, 'and I was the only girl. At the age of seven, I knew how to bake a perfect loaf of bread. I am quite content to be one of the Marthas of this world.'

But I will not go and *live* there, Miss Bartlett told herself, towards the end of that summer. I am determined to remain independent, my plans are fluid, I have my work, and besides, it would never do, we might not get on well together and then it would be embarrassing for me to have to leave. And people might talk.

Though she knew that they would not, and that it was of her own judgement that she was most afraid, for Mountsea was full of ladies of indeterminate age, sharing houses together.

The winter came, and the cottage was indeed damp. The

stone walls struck cold all day and all night, in spite of expensive electric heaters, and Miss Bartlett spent longer and longer afternoons at Tuscany, even taking some of her work up there, from time to time.

At the beginning of December, the first of the bad storms sent waves crashing up over the quayside into the front room.

Of course, Miss Roscommon is lonely, she said now, she has need of me, I should have realized. That type of woman, who appears to be so competent and strong, feels the onset of old age and infirmity more than most, but she cannot say so, cannot give way and confess to human weakness. She bakes me cakes and worries about the dampness in my house because she needs my company and concern for herself.

And so, on Christmas Eve, when the second storm filled Miss Bartlett's living-room with water up to the level of the window seat, she allowed herself to be evacuated by the capable Miss Roscommon up to the white bungalow.

'It will not be for good,' she said anxiously, 'when the weather improves, I shall have to go back, there is the business to be thought of.' 'We shall make plans for a proper shop,' said Miss Roscommon firmly, 'I have a little money...'

She filled up a pottery bowl with leek soup, having acquired her faith in its restorative powers when she had set up a canteen at the scene of a mining disaster in the nineteen-twenties.

Miss Bartlett accepted the soup and a chair close to the fire and an electric blanket for her bed, thereby setting the seal on the future pattern of their relationship. By the beginning of February, plans for the shop were made, by mid-March, the work was in hand. There was no longer any talk of her moving, she would sell her goods from the new shop during the summer days, but she would live at Tuscany. The garage was fitted with light, heat and two extra windows, and made into a studio.

'This is quite the best arrangement,' said Miss Roscommon, 'here, you will be properly fed and looked after, I shall see to that.'

Over the seven years that followed, Miss Bartlett came to rely upon her for many more things than the comforts of a well-kept home. It was Miss Roscommon who made all the business arrangements for the new shop, who saw the bank manager, the estate agent and the builder, Miss Roscommon who advised with the orders and the accounts. During the summer seasons, the shop did well, and after three years, at her friend's suggestion, Miss Bartlett started to make pink raffia angels and pot-pourri jars, for the Christmas postal market.

She relaxed, ceased to feel uneasy, and if, from time to time, she did experience a sudden shot of alarm, at seeing herself so well and truly settled, she said, not, 'Where else would I go?' but, 'I am needed here. However would she manage without me? It would be cruel to go.' All the decisions were left to Miss Roscommon. 'You are so much better at these things . . .' Miss Bartlett said, and drifted away to her studio, a small woman with pastel-coloured flesh.

Perhaps it was her forty-seventh birthday that jolted her into a renewed awareness of her situation. She looked into the mirror on that morning, and saw middle-age settled irrevocably over her features. She was reminded of her dependence upon Miss Roscommon.

I said I would not stay here, she thought, would never have my name written up above a permanent shop, for my plans were to remain fluid. And now it is seven years, and how many opportunities have I missed? How many roads are closed to me?

Or perhaps it was the visit of Miss Roscommon's niece Angela, and her husband of only seven days, one weekend in early September.

'I shall do a great deal of baking,' Miss Roscommon said, 'for they will certainly stay to tea. We shall have cheese scones and preserves and a layer cake.'

'I did not realize that you had a niece.'

Miss Roscommon rose from the table heavily, for she had put on weight, over the seven years. There had also been some suspicion about a cataract in her left eye, another reason why Miss Bartlett told herself she could not leave her.

She is my youngest brother's child. I haven't seen her since she was a baby.'

Miss Bartlett nodded and wandered away from the breakfast table, not liking to ask why there had been no wedding invitation. Even after seven years, Miss Roscommon kept some of her secrets, there were subjects upon which she simply did not speak, though Miss Bartlett had long ago bared her own soul.

The niece Angela, and her new husband, brought a slab of wedding cake, which was put to grace the centre of the table, on a porcelain stand.

'And this,' said Miss Roscommon triumphantly, '*this* is my friend, Miss Mary Bartlett.' For Miss Bartlett had hung behind in the studio for ten minutes after their arrival, out of courtesy and because it was always something of a strain for her to meet new people.

'Mary is very shy, very retiring,' her own mother had always said, 'she is artistic you see, she lives in her own world.' Her tone had always been proud and Miss Bartlett had therefore come to see her own failure to make human relationships as a mark of distinction. Her shyness had been cultivated, readily admitted to.

The niece and her husband sat together on the sofa, a little flushed and self-conscious in new clothes. Seeing them there, Miss Bartlett realized for the first time that no young people had ever been inside the bungalow, since her arrival. But it was more than their youthfulness which struck her, there was an air of suppressed excitement about them, a glitter, they emanated pride in the satisfactions of the flesh.

Miss Roscommon presided over a laden tea-table, her face still flushed from the oven.

'And Miss Bartlett is very clever,' she told them, 'she

makes beautiful things. You must go down to the shop and see them, buy something for your new home.'

'You make things?' said Angela, through a mouthful of shortbread, 'what sort of things?'

Miss Bartlett made a little gesture of dismissal with her hand. 'Oh, not very much really, nothing at all exciting. Just a few little . . . I'm sure you wouldn't . . .' She let her voice trail off, but it was Miss Roscommon and not the niece Angela who took her up on it.

'Now that is just nonsense,' she said firmly. 'There is no virtue in this false modesty, I have told you before. Of course Angela will like your things, why should she not? Plenty of visitors do, and there is nothing to be ashamed of in having a talent.'

'I wore a hand-embroidered dress,' said the niece Angela, 'for my wedding.'

Miss Bartlett watched her, and watched the new husband, whose eyes followed Angela's slim hand as it moved over to the cake plate and back, and up into her mouth. Their eyes met and shone with secrets, across the table. Miss Bartlett's stomach moved a little, with fear and excitement. She felt herself to be within touching distance of some very important piece of knowledge.

'Do you help with this shop, then –?' asked the husband, though without interest.

'Oh, no! Well, here and there with the accounts and so forth, because Mary doesn't understand any of that, she is such a dreamer! No, no, that is not my job, that is not what keeps me so busy. My job is to look after Mary, of course. I took that upon myself quite some time ago, when I saw that I was needed. She is such a silly girl, she lives in a world of her own and if I were not here to worry about her meals and her comforts, she would starve, I assure you, simply starve.'

'Oh, I don't think I really . . .'

'Of course you would,' said Miss Roscommon. 'Now let me have your cup to be filled.'

The young couple exchanged another glance, of comprehension and amusement. How dare you, thought Miss Bartlett, almost in tears with anger and frustration, at being so looked upon and judged and misunderstood. What do you know of it, how can you sit there so smugly? It is because you are young and know nothing. It is all very well for you.

'All the same,' said the niece Angela, sitting back in her chair, 'it's very nice to be looked after. I must say.'

She smiled like a cat.

'Yes, that has always been my role in life, that is *my* talent,' said Miss Roscommon, 'to do all the looking after.' She leaned over and patted Miss Bartlett on the hand. 'She is my responsibility now, you see,' she told them confidently. 'My little pussy-cat.'

Miss Bartlett pushed the hand away and got to her feet, her face flushed with shame and annoyance. 'What a foolish thing to say! Of course I am not, how very silly you make me look. I am a grown woman, I am quite capable of looking after myself.'

Miss Roscommon, not in the least discomfited, only began to pour the tea dregs into a slop basin, smiling.

When they were about to leave, Miss Bartlett said, 'I will walk down the hill with you, and we shall drop in for a minute at the shop. Yes, I insist. . . . But not for you to buy anything. You must choose a wedding present from my stock, it is the very least I can do.' For she wanted to keep them with her longer, to be seen walking in their company down the hill away from the bungalow, wanted to be on their side.

'You will need a warm coat, it is autumn now, the evenings are drawing in. Take your mohair.'

'Oh, leave me, leave me, do not *fuss*.' And Miss Bartlett walked to the end of the gravelled drive, while the niece and her new husband made their good-byes.

'I am afraid it is all she has to worry over nowadays,' she said hastily, the moment they had joined her. 'It gives her pleasure, I suppose, to do all that clucking round and I have not the heart to do anything but play along, keep up appearances. If it were not for me, she would be so lonely. Of course, I have had to give up a good deal of my own life, on that account.'

The niece Angela took her husband's arm. 'It must be very nice and comfortable for you there,' she said, 'all the same.'

Miss Bartlett turned her face away and looked out to sea. Another winter, she thought, and I am now forty-seven years old. You do not understand.

She detained them in the shop for as long as possible, fetching out special items from the stock room and taking time over the wrapping paper. Let me be with you, she wanted to say, let me be on your side, for do you not see that I still have many opportunities left, I am not an old woman, I know about the world and the ways of modern life. Take me with you.

But when they had gone she stood in the darkening shop and saw that they had already placed and dismissed her, that she did not belong with them and there was no hope left. She sat on the stool beside the till and wept, for the injustice of the world and the weakness of her own nature. I have become what I always dreaded becoming, she said, everything has slipped through my fingers.

And for all of it, after a short time, she began to blame Miss Roscommon. She has stifled me, she thought, she preys upon me, I am treated as her child, her toy, her *pussy-cat*, she has humiliated me and fed off my dependence and the fact that I have always been so sensitive. She is a wicked woman. And then she said, *but I do not have to stay with her*. Fortified by the truth of this new realization, Miss Bartlett blew her nose, and walked back up the hill to Tuscany.

'You cannot leave,' said Miss Roscommon, 'what nonsense, of course you cannot. You have nowhere else to go and besides, in ten days' time we set off for our holiday in Florence.'

'You will set off. I am afraid my plans have now changed.' Miss Bartlett could not now bear the thought of being seen with her friend in all the museums and art galleries of Florence, discussing the paintings in loud, knowledgeable voices and eating wholemeal sandwiches out of neat little greaseproof bags, speaking very slowly to the Italians. This year Miss Roscommon must go alone. She did not allow herself to think of how, or whether she would enjoy herself. We are always hearing of how intrepid she was as a girl, she thought. Then let her be intrepid again.

Aloud, she said, 'I am going back to live at the cottage.' For she had kept it on, and rented it to summer visitors.

Miss Roscommon turned herself, and her darning, a little more towards the light. 'You are being very foolish,' she said mildly. 'But I understand why, it is your age, of course.'

Appalled, Miss Bartlett went through to her room, and began to throw things furiously, haphazardly, into a suitcase. I am my own mistress, she said, a grown-up woman with years ahead of me, it is time for me to be firm. I have pandered to her long enough.

The following day, watched by Miss Roscommon, she moved back down the hill to the cottage. She would, she decided, stay there for a while, give herself time to get accustomed, and to gather all of her things around her again, and then she would look out and make plans, take steps towards her new life.

That evening, hearing the wind around her own four walls, she said, I have escaped. Though she woke in the night and was aware of being entirely alone in the cottage, of not being able to hear the loud breathing of Miss Roscommon in the room next door.

She expected the Italian holiday to be cancelled, on some pretext, and was astonished when Miss Roscommon left, on the appointed day and alone. Miss Bartlett took the opportunity of going up to Tuscany and fetching some more of her things down, work from the studio to keep her busy in the evening, and during the days, too, for now it was October and few people came into the shop.

Here I am, she said, twisting the raffia angels and winding ribbon around the pot-pourris, etching her gift cards, here I am, living my own life and making my own decisions. She wanted to invite someone down to stay, someone young, so that she could be seen and approved of, but there was no one. A search through all the drawers and cupboards at the bungalow did not yield her the address of the niece Angela. She would have sent a little note, with a Christmas gift, to tell of her removal, prove her independence.

Miss Roscommon returned from Italy, looking rather tired and not very suntanned. She came in with a miniature plaster copy of a Donatello statue, and some fine art post-cards. Miss Bartlett made tea, and the conversation was very stilted.

'You are not warm enough here,' said Miss Roscommon, 'I will send down some extra blankets.'

'Oh no, thank you. Please don't do that.'

But the following day the blankets, and a Dutch apple pie, arrived with the butcher's boy.

Miss Bartlett bought huge slabs of cheese and eggs, which she could boil quite well, and many potatoes, and ate them off her knee while she read detective stories through the long evenings. She thought that she might buy a television set for company, though she was busy too, with the postal orders for Christmas. When all this is over, she told herself, that is when I shall start looking about me and making my plans. She thought of all the things she might have done as a girl, the studio in London and the woodblock engravings for the poetry press, the ballet company for whom she might have been asked to do some ethereal costume designs. She read in a newspaper of a woman who had started her own firm, specializing in computer management, at the age of fifty and was now rather wealthy, wholly respected in a man's world. Miss Bartlett looked at herself in the mirror. I am only forty-seven, she said.

In her white bungalow, lonely and lacking a sense of purpose, Miss Roscommon waited.

On November the seventh, the first of the storms came, and Miss Bartlett sat in her back room and heard the wind and the crashing of the sea, terrified. The next morning, she saw that part of the pierhead had broken away. Miss Roscommon sent down a note, with a meat pasty, via the butcher's boy.

'I am worried about you,' she wrote, 'you cannot be looking after yourself, and I know that it is damp in that cottage. Your room here is ready for you at any time.'

Miss Bartlett tore the note up and threw the pasty away, but she thought of the warm bed, the fires and soft sofas at Tuscany.

Two days later, when the gales began again, Miss Roscommon came herself, and hammered at the door of the cottage, but Miss Bartlett hid upstairs, behind a cheval mirror, until she went away. This time, there was no note, only a thermos flask of lentil soup on the doorstep.

She is suffocating me, thought Miss Bartlett, I cannot bear all these unwanted attentions, I only wish to be left alone. It is a poor thing if a woman of her age and resources can find nothing else to occupy her, nothing else to live for. But in spite of herself, she drank the soup, and the taste of it, the smell of the steam rising up into her face, reminded her of all the meals at Tuscany, the winter evenings spent happily sitting beside the fire.

When the storms came again, another section of the pier broke away, the lifeboat put out to sea and sank with all hands, and the front room of Miss Bartlett's cottage was flooded, rain broke in through a rent in the roof. She lay all night, too terrified by the roaring of the wind and seas, to get out of bed and do anything about it, only whimpering a little with cold and fright, remembering how close the cottage came to the water, how vulnerable she was.

As a child, she had been afraid of all storms, gales and thunder and cloudbursts drumming on the roof, and her mother had understood, wrapped her in a blanket and taken her into her own bed.

'It is because you have such a vivid imagination,' she had said, 'you feel things that the other, ordinary little children, cannot ever feel.' And so, nothing had been done to conquer this praiseworthy fear of storms.

Now, I am alone, thought Miss Bartlett, there is no one, my mother is dead, and who is there to shelter and understand me? A flare rocket, sent up from the sinking lifeboat, lit up the room faintly for a second, and then she knew who there was, and that everything would be all right. On the stormy nights, Miss Roscommon always got up and made sandwiches and milky hot drinks, brought them to her as she lay awake in bed, and they would sit reading nice magazines, in the gentle circle of the bedside lamp.

I have been very foolish, Miss Bartlett thought, and heard herself saying it aloud, humbly, to Miss Roscommon. A very foolish, selfish woman, I do not deserve to have you as a friend.

She did not take very much with her up the hill on the following morning, only a little handcase and some raffia work. The rest could follow later, and it would be better to arrive like that, it would be a real indication of her helplessness.

The landscape was washed very clean and bare and pale, but the sea churned and moved within itself, angry and battleship grey. In the summer, Miss Bartlett thought, refreshed again by the short walk, it will be time to think again, for I am not committing myself to any permanent arrangement and things will have to be rather different now, I will not allow myself to be treated as a pet plaything, that must be understood. For she had forgotten, in the cold, clear morning, the terrors of the previous night.

She wondered what to do, ring the bell or knock or simply open the back door into the kitchen, where Miss Roscommon would be working, and stand there, case in hand, waiting to be forgiven. Her heart beat a little faster. Tuscany was very settled and reassuring in its low, four-square whiteness on top of the hill. Miss Bartlett knocked timidly at the blue kitchen door.

It was some time before she gave up knocking and ringing, and simply went in. Tuscany was very quiet.

She found her in the living-room, lying crumpled up awkwardly on the floor, one of her legs twisted underneath her. Her face was a curious, flat colour, like the inside of a raw potato. Miss Bartlett drew back the curtains. The clock had stopped just before midnight, almost twelve hours ago.

For a moment, she stood there, still holding her little case, in the comfortable, chintzy room, and then she dropped down on to her knees, and took the head of Miss Roscommon into her lap and, rocking and rocking, cradling it like a child, Miss Bartlett wept.

Yehuda Amichai

Battle for the Hill

Translated by Hillel Halkin

*This story is set in Jerusalem during the Sinai Campaign of 1956
when the city, protected by thousands of suddenly mobilized
citizen-soldiers, waited five long days for a war which never came.
The title is itself an ironic comment on the countless war stories with
similar names which have filled Israel's periodicals during the
past two decades.*

My wife and I crossed the street which led to where our
friends live. We passed by the leper hospital, but as usual I
failed to see a single one of the white invalids among the
old trees. You never see them. The gates are always open,
footsteps have trodden the grass and wheels have flattened
it, but one never sees a soul. Sometimes you see milk cans
standing before one of the iron doors sunk deep within the
wall. I have yet to see a milkman.

One day last winter I stood beside this same wall and
took refuge from a sudden cloudburst. I stood under the
small corrugated roof which projects from it at an angle.
I have no idea why the slanting roof was built. I stood
fixed beneath it like a holy icon in some Christian land.
Standing there, I watched the last fugitives fleeing from
the rain and listened to the noise they made as they splashed
through the puddles.

Now, however, a soldier stood near the wall. I watched
him gesture with his hands as if he were directing traffic.
There were no cars within sight or hearing, but I spotted a

young woman crossing a field covered with rocks and briars. The soldier motioned to her with his hands, and I heard him call out: 'More to the right, that's it, and now to the left again. No, no! Not towards me. Away from me. That's right, that's right.' The woman obeyed his directions, growing smaller until she disappeared; I doubt if she will ever see him again, or if he will see her.

Our friends live on a plot of land which is not theirs and in a house which is not theirs. The armchair in the living-room has finally been repaired, and the bay window is at rest at last. It is recessed and placid, like a gulf into which ships no longer venture. For the first time in years the iron gate was open. The wash was hung out to dry; shirts and pants swayed freed of the body, like our thoughts, which are formed in our bodies but sometimes fly free in the wind. My friend's wife runs a kindergarten. The front yard contained a playground: a slide and a tiny ladder for make-believe angels. The children push and shove each other until they reach the top. The pleasure of sliding down lasts no longer than a second. A small boy, who seemed to have been forgotten from the day before, stood there holding a red balloon in his hands. An old car, stripped of its wheels and motor and painted red, rested in the sand for the children to play with. In a like manner the ideas of my fore-fathers have come down to me: just the frame with a bright coat of paint. Sometimes it seems that I sit in them, or play with them, but I never go anywhere.

The army runner came looking for me. The same soldier I had seen giving directions to his wife turned out to be the runner of my company, who had been dispatched to bring me in. He is always on the run, with some message in his hand or mouth. Now I spied him coming down the walled-in road. A piece of white paper fluttered in his hands like a captured butterfly. He caught up with me as I stood in the playground beside the painted car. Gasping and panting he halted before me short of breath, looking the way runners are supposed to look. I read what was written on the paper.

Instead of going on to see our friends, I sat my wife down in the sand box next to the forgotten boy, and proceeded to the mobilization room at the army base. I passed through many rooms: the buffet, the engineering corps room, the synagogue, the quartermaster's room, the bathroom – until finally I came to the mobilization room. There I expected to find a great bustle of people, coming and going in a hurry, but I found only two women soldiers sitting in front of the door. 'Wait just a minute!' they said in unison as I approached, and then settled down again. One of them wore a blouse with a flower pattern and a khaki shirt, the other a khaki blouse and a skirt with a flower pattern – like clowns at Purim. It had all happened suddenly. One of them had been on leave and had just had time to put on her khaki blouse again when there came a knock on her front door. The other was preparing to go on leave and had already removed her army skirt when they knocked on *her* door. In the confusion she had snatched the skirt with the flower pattern that was draped over the back of a chair, and had put it on, holding it tight with both hands because she couldn't find the zipper.

'We weren't expecting this.'

'We weren't ready.'

'Can I go in now?'

'One moment. What's the rush? You'll get there.'

'We weren't ready. It happened so suddenly.'

'It always comes suddenly.'

'The bottom of your slip is showing.'

'I know. It's too long for the khaki skirt.'

'When I'm in uniform, I don't wear my slip.'

'Too bad.'

'We just weren't ready.'

Then I heard the sound of chairs being moved about inside the room. Distant doors opened and slammed shut, and heavy footsteps resounded through the building.

'You can enter now. Come in!' said a voice from within.

It was getting on towards evening. The last rays of sun-

shine slanted through the drawn blinds, staining my forehead with a golden light. I wiped the stains from my
forehead like beads of sweat, and entered. My captain sat at
the table and did not bother to turn around. He was surrounded by maps on every side. On one of them lay a pair
of eyeglasses. A second pair he wore. I have never been
able to make up my mind whether I like him or hate him.
Watching him once during target practice, I saw him
remove his glasses, and noticed that there was sadness in his
eyes. Ever since then he has risen in my esteem. Now he
continued to bend over the table, still without turning
around. Like the Roman god Janus, he had two faces.
Bristling with tiny hairs and unaware of the future, the
expressionless face of his neck looked towards me, while the
face which had eyes and a nose looked towards the map. It is
my belief that if there is an end to this universe and if there
is a God, there is also a gigantic neck, the face of which
looks out towards the space beyond and is never seen. The
captain's neck said to me:

'Sit down, sit down. I'll be with you in a minute.'

'I left my wife in the sand box.'

'You did well.'

'By the monkey bars and the slide. The tea will get
cold.'

'Come have a look at the photograph.'

I came closer but saw nothing. I held the dark paper up
against the evening light and saw that it was an X-ray.
They had taken an X-ray of the entire location and of the
hill. A strange bone had gotten into it, however, and I saw
all my sadness and the negative of my white wife sitting in
the sand box beneath the clothes-line. A breeze sprang up
and papers rustled and fell to the floor. Tea was brought,
and I placed my glass upon the map. 'The tea is exactly
over the objective,' said my captain. 'The point we have to
capture is underneath your glass.'

Afterwards he entrusted me with a list of the names
of those who had to be assembled. 'You have to tell them

when to leave their homes. Synchronize your watch with mine. You have to begin everything from the end. In reverse. But to return to the present moment, perhaps one should draw up the battle order to cover the past too, as far back as kindergarten: the attack, the final preparations, the good-bye to the wife, the last kiss, inspection of the boots, the next to the last good-bye; hopes and delusions; 'relative' peace, marriage, study, a course in communications and breaking of communications, a course in love and disappointment, father dies in the night, school, kindergarten; there you have your battle order and the calendar in reverse,' laughed my captain. We stood by the window, and he rested his arm on my shoulder. 'In retrospect, in retrospect,' he said. . .

I went to the buffet; my wife sat in the corner over a glass of yellow juice, a straw in her mouth. She did not drink; rather, the glass seemed to drink her. As on those moonlit nights, when she grows diffuse and becomes sad and empty and cannot sleep, I held on to the back of her hands, which held on to the cold glass. The small, lithe girls, wriggling in their dresses behind the counter, signalled to me that they wished to close the room for the night. The room will be closed. The world will be closed. The buffet will grow dark; the world will grow dark. As soon as my wife fell asleep I rose to my feet and left. From here on we shall grow accustomed to strange good-byes. By the glass, by the white pillow, by the door and by all the other strange places. They are lucky, these soldiers who are shipped across the great sea; the awful ripping of paper in every good-bye is swallowed by the tremulous onrush of the waves. Here a great noise is needed to still the voice of my wife in the house next door, behind the front line. My life has always been either the noise before the stillness or the stillness before the noise. Between them I can get no rest. Will it be noisy or still, I wonder, when death comes to take me? . . .

The company clerk came and handed me the mobilization slips, as if it were a lottery. I went about the city, waking my friends so that they might gird themselves for battle. It was not always easy to do this by myself. Later I lost a number of my men. I distributed the white slips. Some were crammed through cracks in the doors like whispering snakes. Children babbled in their sleep. I answered them wakefully and they lapsed into silence. Cars cruised quietly by, secretly sliding around corners. Grown men cried. The eucalyptus tree had insomnia; it shook all over. Each leaf was an open, smarting eye. One day, when there is peace, I shall place a eucalyptus branch where my heavy heart now lies. I stretched my hand into no-man's land and touched a piece of paper thrown by the enemy. A midnight wind blew through the fragments of bottles. To confuse the enemy I sped to the other end of town. A woman stood in a doorway in a vacant lot and said, 'He's not home, he's not home!' I heard the water being flushed in the bathroom; her husband emerged drunk with sleep, following after me as in the tale of the golden goose: whoever touches its feathers is caught fast, and must go along with it, no matter what.

I turned off my flashlight; the beam returned like a well-trained dog. We descended to the cellar, where the smell of poverty and children's sleep greeted my nostrils. But my friend was already standing before me in uniform, his pack slung over his shoulder. 'What do you have in that pack?' 'I don't know.' His forehead was pale and deeply lined, like stairs which have been walked on a great deal. His wife stood behind me dressed in a billowy white robe. 'Don't mind her,' he said. She is dying already, and every evening at midnight she will appear to him. The woman faded from sight, and in her place came the steps, as white as she had been.

The roosters cry all through the night, not only at dawn. I cannot sleep the whole night long and during the day I dream. Dreams hovered above the city like vapour from a hot drink. Water flowed through every drainpipe on every roof. A single car shot off in several directions. Like my head: only my mouth remained stationary and refused to run about as did the other parts of my face. Men received instructions like police cars and shifted direction. I slipped away from the soldiers who were rounding up the company, and went off to the buffet to fetch my wife. I woke the officer on duty. Sleeping soldiers littered the lawns and footpaths. I opened the door of the buffet. My wife was slumped over a tabletop, sticky with old candy, still gripping her glass. I picked her up, the glass clutched in her hand. Light struck it and it shimmered. On the way out my wife slipped from my grasp and fell, breaking the glass. My wife banged her head. She didn't even groan, and I became frightened. We sat together by the roadside. You could hear the frog-talk over the wireless in the radio car. I carried my wife home and put her to bed.

'Did you pick up the broken glass?'

'I picked it up and now I have to go.'

'Why? Where to?'

'I took it you knew.'

'Once you said "I take you to be my wedded wife," and we broke a glass then too.'

'Once we sat by a white wall with vines on it.'

'My head hurts.'

'Because you fell. Soon it will be dawn. Do you hear a car?'

'Yes.'

'They're coming for me.'

'No, it's the milkman.'

'No, it's the army car that's coming for me.'

I packed my shirts and a few pairs of underwear. The time I had allotted to myself was up. The vehicle which passed was not the milk truck, and it was not for me. I took my belongings. When I opened my neatly pressed white handkerchief to wipe my brow, I saw that printed upon it was a plan of the enemy hill: a lonely tumble-down shack, and next to it a number of well-fortified positions. My name was embroidered below: the first initials of my name in the corner of the handkerchief which bore the plan. The approaches were indicated by arrows, the artillery emplacement by crosses or circles. I folded the handkerchief without wiping my brow. I saw that my wife was sleeping. I saw the pieces of broken glass in the street and went out. On the stairway, I switched on the light to look at the handkerchief again. What was the hill called? From where would we attack? How would we set up the light machine-guns, and where would we evacuate the wounded and through what conduit in the world would all the blood flow? The long-destined hill. The ultimate hill. I have heard that the sun rises in the East. I heard the first pedestrians in the streets and I hoped that my wife would sleep on and on. I folded the handkerchief lovingly and put it away. I drank a cup of coffee standing up, without sensing the taste of war. New death notices had been put up on the bulletin board. There were also posters calling on the residents of different cities to assemble for memorial rallies in honour of the six million. In all probability these were mobilization calls in disguise. The newspaper fell from my hands and I let it lie.

A car drove up and stopped near me: 'Come with me.' 'Where are you going? You're not from the army?' The driver laughed and said, 'Don't you see the way I've smeared the windshields with mud?' The earth is rising. The fragrance of the earth is rising. He then showed me pictures of his children. 'Where are we going?' He held his hand up before my eyes and said, 'Here is the map, we will follow the lines on my palm.' The water swashed about in his canteen. 'Soon we will be home again,' I said to calm him. Like my mother, who used to calm us by saying about everything that it was nothing. If it was blistering hot she said, 'Just another summer day.' When it hailed she said, 'How pleasant the air is, so mild and fresh! It's good that it's not too dry. It's good there is no drought.'

The strings from which I dangled like a marionette in a puppet show became entwined and tangled among other strings; when somebody else was supposed to move I moved instead, and vice versa. And all the time the voice fixed above our heads continued to talk. I asked the driver to stop, and I went to call one of the men in my company who lived in a large courtyard; the passageway was still sealed off with the branches of trees that had broken during the winter. Over the door was a sheet of paper with the names of all the tenants. Next to each name was written how many times to ring. I rang four times. I waited, but the door did not open. I watched the open army trucks pass by, decked out with the long hair of girls, with antennas and machine guns. Although I knew that there was still time, I hid behind the door. I heard footsteps approaching. The door opened. A man saw me and turned pale; he then returned to his room to put on his glasses. Then he begged my pardon for the delay in opening the door; he didn't know if it was ringing for him. Sometimes it rings four times and it's not for him. During his vacations he lies on his back and counts the number of rings. He is always waiting. He has often been mistaken. He has often been mistaken in his life. He is a teacher and there are stacks of notebooks in his room, filled with red marks correcting students' mistakes. Like his life. In his room is a single window, and the blinds are generally lowered. He finished arranging his things and came with me. Civilian cars which had been commandeered for the war passed by, camouflaged with mud and dark blankets.

Towards evening I was assigned to observe the hill with the shack for the first time. I entered a house which stood near the border. The stairway was empty and the plaster was peeling from the walls, on which a few mail boxes hung. In one box the letters overflowed. The tenant was long gone, but the letters continued to arrive. Sometimes, when I have wandered far in my thoughts, people speak to me and their words clutter the gateways to my being without penetrating any further, because I do not choose to admit them.

I went up to the top floor. A woman wiping her hands on an apron let me in. I showed her the letter from the army. Domestic odours permeated the house. A pressure burner chattered noisily. A girl sang in the bathtub and soap bubbles popped all over her – but I was unable to see. My heart welled up within me, and all the words which had accumulated in my head like letters in the abandoned mail box suddenly fell and glutted my heart instead. I recalled my mission and my eyes grew bleary with worry, like the camouflaged windshields which were smeared with mud. A boy stood and stared at me. I formed an arch over him like the vault of the skies, the worries smudged my eyes. The boy's mouth was smudged with food. I ascended to the attic. I lay down between the wooden crates with the boy at my feet. 'What are you looking at?' he asked. 'At the years to come,' I answered, 'and at my wife lying in bed because her head is broken.' The boy left; I heard his laugh from a distance. My captain was already at the window. The wire screen was in our way. We ripped it apart and were deluged by dust. My captain passed me the binoculars.

'Do you see that ridge? Do you see that line, that elevation, that trench, that point?' I saw them, and we compared them with the map. The world was exact and efficient. My captain got up to go. 'Stay a while,' he said to me, 'and take notes on whatever you see.' I took notes: A man went by with his donkey. A man went by with his wife. The sun is slowly setting. A man is stretching himself by the shack and lifting his two arms. To whom is he surrendering?

I heard footsteps behind me. The boy returned and began to ask questions. I gave him pencil and paper and told him to draw the hill. He drew the hill with himself standing on it. He drew a flag and a ball rolling down the slope. More officers arrived to take their first glimpse of the lonely outpost. I returned by way of the apartment. The bathroom door was open and the burner had stopped chattering. I asked permission to wash my hands. The girl whose voice I had heard before stood in front of me. 'Why are you staring at me like a dummy?' she said. 'Help me dry my back!' I took the towel and massaged her skin until it turned red.

'What did you do up there in the attic?' she asked.

'We looked.'

'Did you see my old dolls?'

'I'll come back.'

'My back is already dry. Now on your way!'

She laughed, tossing her thick black hair. Her eyes sparkled and her mouth was red. Drops of water from her hair fell on to my khaki shirt and dried instantly. Her snub nose was fresh and provoking. She caught me by the ears and said, 'You're coming back, you're coming back to me!' After seeing her, I couldn't go straight back to the army, so I took a roundabout route by way of the valleys which encircle the city. The Spanish consul drove past in his automobile. The consul of chaos hoisted his ensign. Jews gathered in the Orthodox quarter of Mea Shearim to cry 'Ma'ariv Ma'ariv,'* their faces turned towards an east which is no longer the East. East is the magnetic pole of the Jews. I glanced at my watch and saw that it was time to be in the school building for the parents' meeting; I sat in the teachers' lounge and waited for the parents to arrive. Whatever way you look at it, there is no helping the parents and no preventing bloodshed on the hill with the shack. Only time can occasionally intervene and permit life to linger on a little longer. Bergman stuck his head in the door to see if I had come. One of his children is alive and the other is dead. The dead child is lobbying for him in the world to come. He has already made inroads among the dead; he is an honorary consul in heaven. The child who is still living studies with me. Bergman was with me in the army during the Second World War. Now he sat silently before me. In

*'Ma'ariv' is the Jewish daily evening prayer. Literally, the word means 'evening', and is related to the word 'ma'arav', which means 'west'.

the glass cabinet there stood the physics apparatus: pieces that interlock, for example, though we never interlock; or the lead ball, which after being heated cannot pass through the ring because it no longer fits. There were also shells from Elath in which you could listen to the sea, and a paper world glued to a globe, very like the world glued to the head on my shoulders, which is also nearly round.

The sister of one of my pupils approached me; she was already grown up and married. One of her eyes she fixed on me; the other was blind and white, with the eyeball turned inward. Ageing fathers came who failed to recognize their own sons: 'Which one do you mean, which one do you mean, Yosef or Shmuel?' Fathers resemble their sons and everybody resembles everybody, and we are all enemies nonetheless. I placed the plan of the hill beside my grade book, and from time to time I peeked at it. Beneath the grades for discipline, for good behaviour and arithmetic, were the dotted lines which stood for the enemy positions. I had been informed that my company was not to be held responsible for capturing the entire hill, but only for its southern slope. Beyond that there remained a few dirt embankments, and a handful of enemy soldiers sitting behind them. When we really attack it will not be necessary to pin numbers on our backs like basketball players to avoid mistaking one side for the other; we won't make mistakes. And if we do, that too is ultimately no mistake. In the meantime much was happening: The sun set. Children screamed. A wind blew. Dust came and the window was shut. As in the Book of Job, one messenger was followed by another. The teacher, Miss Ziva, had arrived.

'We're on to you, we know all about you.'

I covered the plan with my hand so that Ziva should not see it. It was forbidden for security reasons.

'We know all about you, all about the girl whose back you wiped.'

Miss Ziva has read widely and is an expert on weather conditions and the heavenly winds. She is prettier in winter than in summer. Someone's father stepped forward and complained that his son was noisy and unruly, that he coloured the walls of the house all the colours of the sunset, that he threw stones at cats and dogs and was spoiling his mother's dreams.

Miss Ziva was irritated. 'Why don't you give them some advice?' Her eyes are as hard as metal screws. Once she wanted to rivet herself to the world with those eyes, but she didn't succeed. Once we went for a walk in the fields, her nylon stockings ripped on a thornbush, and she became angry with me. To this day she traverses the world with those hard blue eyes. Why had she come to me?

I was being called from the street. 'Wait just a minute,' I said, 'one more mother.' 'I can't begin to tell you,' said the mother when she came, 'what a nuisance my naughty girl has been to me ever since she lay in my belly.'

Bergman went off to an adjoining room to chat with the other teachers. The shadows under his eyes were like the shadows cast by a cloud that refuses to pass. His wife must say to him, 'You have to get ahead in the world!' So he gets ahead, but the cloud beneath his eyes recalls him to the starting point. Bergman is a surveyor; what does he do? He goes out every morning and plants his black and white rods deep in the waste and, gazing into the distance like a prophet: here will be houses, here will be gardens and cemeteries! I, on the other hand, have to prophesy about the men who will live in these houses. He always has his queer equipment about him. His poles, his theodolite, his scrolls, his registers, his calculations.

Bergman unbuttoned his overcoat to show me how his lapel was torn like a mourner's. Then he unbuttoned his shirt and took out his undershirt. I saw that even his chest bore the print of dried mud, just like the transports. 'You see,' he said to me, 'I too.' Men used to sprinkle ashes on their heads as a sign of mourning; now they cake themselves with earth because of the war. Bergman rearranged his clothing and left me with the globe, whose surface had peeled away with the years. A compass and a ruler hung from a hook: these delude the children no less than the teachers, because they foster the illusion that there is really such a thing as a straight line and a pure angle. The picture of the living President stared at the picture of the dead President. The picture of Bialik hung aslant and I straightened it. My favourite pupil entered the room. I patted her on the cheek, smudging her complexion with earth, like Bergman's chest and the cars. 'What fun it will be,' she said to me happily, 'now I too can go to your war!'

When I left, it was already night and my wife was waiting for me at the bottom of the stairs. How did she know I was here? Her hair rustled and the briars rustled and there was a smell of burning in the air and her eyes grew black like after the Great Fire. 'Come,' I said to her, 'we will go wake up some men so that the army may be brought up to full strength.' The first person on our list was a milkman, whose hallway smelt of milk. We entered the courtyard; there are no longer many like it in Jerusalem. By the entrance there once lived an old professor from Czechoslovakia who came here with the escaping Czech army. How he came to be a professor and how he arrived here with the army, I don't know. He lived in a decrepit structure which had one wall adjacent to a ceramics kiln. He was always worrying that this house might go up in flames. He was feeble and emaciated like a dwarf, and though he dwelt above the ground, he lived, as dwarfs do, in the subterranean caverns of his soul. His voice was high and quavering like that of a mouse. Besides him, there lived in the old house an ancient bookbinder, whose sons were scattered about the world. While they drifted over the face of the earth as if swept by gusts of wind, he stuck to his post and fussily tended his books. His two youngest sons were arrested by the British police at the door of his bindery for illegal possession of weapons. The owner of the house was an Armenian doctor who lived in the Old City. Tall, thin and sharp-featured, he put in an appearance every now and then. There was also a storage bin for green vegetables, and sacks of peanuts and more vegetables were piled in a small courtyard.

One room was always rented to independent young girls, the kind who come to Jerusalem to study at the Music Conservatory or at the Bezalel Art School, and take up rug weaving or work in ceramics. They are always independent. When it suits their mood they have a gentleman caller, and when it suits their mood otherwise they kick him out through the courtyard. All day long they are always laundering something. On the top floor was a small school for little girls: the floorboards above the rooms creak with footsteps all day and sharp screams punctuate the recesses. Once I sat in one of those rooms and held an eight-day-old baby on my knees, held him forcibly because he was being circumcised. Afterwards there were little cakes and neighbours, and the wine flowed forlornly into the guests and into that sea which is the receptacle for everything.

My friend the soldier, whom I wished to remind of his military duty, sat by the potter's wheel. He was a potter and worked with clay. Behold the potter in the hands of his clay, I thought to myself. I reversed all the proverbs I knew, and I saw that nothing ever changed in this world. You can bury the living and quicken the dead and nothing will change. 'Wait a moment,' said the soldier, 'I want to finish this pitcher.' The shelves along the wall were lined with scores of pitchers waiting to dry. Much time and much quiet ripening is needed for anything to be finished and perfect. In wartime, however, the unfinished is taken along with the finished, the dry with the wet. Boys are promoted to the rank of adults and ripen too quickly. Whoever breaks, breaks, and those who return no longer have the patience to sit and await their turn like those pitchers. They want to be useful and functional right away. They want a coat of glaze before they are even dry. Later, when the cracks begin to appear, they will be irreparable.

The potter took his rifle from underneath his bed and

began to clean it: the barrel and the breechblock and the two sights, far and near. I have seen many sights in my life. I told him where to go and departed. I waited at the bus stop with my wife. The bus came and she got on. The doors shut and she reached for her fare. She handed the driver a large bill and he had to stop his vehicle and give her change. All her life she has paid for everything with large bills. She sat by the window, resting her head against the back of the seat. The bus lurched forward and disappeared, and she shouted something at me from the window which I couldn't make out. Her speech is like a patch of cloud. When will the rain come? I was overcome by a terrible fear that soon I would be lying mangled and in need of patching on the field adjoining the hill.

I decided to go to the observation post to see the hill by night. I came to the house. A bicycle leaned against the door. Whose was it? The girl stood in the doorway and said, 'I knew you would come.'

'Perhaps you want your back wiped?'

'You have a dirty mind. Have you got a cigarette?'

'I don't smoke. What are you trying to do to me?'

'I'm not doing anything to you.'

'Why are you wearing a red skirt?'

I tried to get past but she wouldn't let me: Don't look at your hill, look at me! I forced my way and she clung to me. I broke free and manacled her with the bicycle lock. 'Don't go away,' I said, 'don't go, soon I'll be down again.' I climbed the stairs to another apartment which was unoccupied and bored through the wall until I could see. The hill was bathed in moonlight. I saw shadowy men shovelling earth like gravediggers; the sound of metal striking against stone reverberated through the air. I added some lines and semicircles to my map, while on a separate slip of paper I wrote: assembly point, evacuation route, two machine guns, preliminary range finding, searchlights, ammunition crates in the small yard. I jotted down a few more notes in the same fashion. When I came downstairs the girl was still standing there, but the bicycle chain was broken. She doesn't know that all will be destroyed.

'Even though I broke loose, I waited for you.' She stood like a heavy white cloud in the darkness.

'There isn't a chance in the world,' I said to her.

'What are those clouds for?'

'The Nile is overflowing its banks.'

'The Nile overflows its banks every year. Why don't you have any children? I'd come and be their nurse.' She kept me company to the top of the street where we were stopped by a soldier hiding in a bread truck. I gave the password and we went on. Afterwards, I walked her home, and we stood on either side of the clothes-line. Her black sleeveless dress had been hung up to dry. It was inside-out, and she stood beside it very sure of herself.

'How old are you?'

'Seventeen.'

'Such a big girl, and your navel hasn't even healed yet.'

'Silly boy, would you like to take a look?'

'Your navel has healed, but your eyes have not healed. After the separation your eyes will never heal. Once you were in the womb of the world. When you came forth and they cut your cord you were separated, and were no longer part of it. That's why you long for it, and your eyes have not healed.' She laughed and fended me off with her hand: 'Go on, go on, you and your maps and your plans.' 'It's because the plans are as sad as my face,' I said to her. 'Your face, my dear, has no sadness and no plans and is unprepared for the future.'

A sergeant passed by. 'Walk along with me,' he said, 'I have to get my army boots.' His army boots were in storage where his old father and mother live. He himself is married and has children and a home of his own, but he leaves his army boots with his parents. His old mother brought him a ladder. He went up to the attic and disappeared there to search. His mother looked at me. 'Why are they calling you?' she asked. I shrugged my shoulders.

Battle for the Hill

That night signs of the impending battle multiplied in the blacked-out city. Cars drove through the streets at a whisper, children ceased to shout. My wife took in the wash from the roof; women soldiers dressed in pyjamas stood by the antennas and spoke into space. Work tools were readied in the cemeteries, and secret arsenals were opened in grocery stores and beneath monuments and sleeping men. Outdoors, human chains passed crates from hand to hand in the square. Jews maddened by the Psalms stood in courtyards, trumpeters and drummers practised in the youth centres. Proclamations were pasted to human backs. Rams' horns were tested, and new machinery and freshly lubricated hopes were brought out into the open. Arms were cached underground. Hearts were tested. Soldiers rested beneath their blankets in driveways, like candleless dead. Queues formed before the cinemas, men picked each other clean of memories, like old notices stripped from a bulletin board, in order to be ready and not weighed down by past events. At the entrance to the city, each citizen received the Insignia of the Holy Earth. Man and his engines preserve Thou, O Lord! Ambulances drove by masked with flapping nets, like the veils on the Bride of Death. Women blessed the Sabbath candles though it was only a weekday. Girls in hoop skirts parachuted in the public squares. Metallic sounds filled the air. Commands were whispered. Loudspeakers were set up. Silent speakers frightened the sleepers.

The following day kindergarten children were driven to the border and told to dance and play for the sake of camouflage. Young girls were brought and told to wear colourful clothing with bright buttons for the sake of camouflage. In the evening pairs of lovers were transported and told to make love before the enemy's eyes for the sake of camouflage, so that the enemy might not see the preparations for the terrible battle.

My captain came and said, 'We have to find another house from which we can see the southern side of the hill.'

We circled the hill like Balaam and Balak. 'Just a minute,' I said, 'just a minute.' My wife's hand was firmly in my own. Big hands must hold little hands: this is their duty in the world. My wife looked at my captain with hostility. 'I too have left my wife and children,' he said. My captain showed us pictures of his wife and children. They smiled the way people smile on the pictures you find in the pockets of dead soldiers. We approached the sentry, who was our grocer, but was now guarding the way. 'Your wife can go no further,' he said; 'from here on the front begins.' He gave her a jar of yogurt, some plum jelly and a few other provisions, and she went home. She was too weighed down to turn around, but I watched her go. It was well that she had her hands full with the jars she was carrying. From here on I was deeply engrossed in conversation with my captain.

'They've added four new positions during the night.'

'And they've added rolls of barbed wire there, a whole sea of barbed wire, and mines near the red house in the southern valley.'

'This will be our assembly point. It has water, drainage and sewerage. It has an exit and an entrance to the world.'

'Where will we set up the machine guns?'

'Many will fall.'

A Yemenite boy came along and we bought two sticks of ice cream from him. We sucked them until only the sticks were left. We took the sticks and traced out a map on the ground, pointing with them as one does with the pointer of a Torah scroll. More officers joined the conference. They all scratched lines and dots in the ground, manipulating little stones and bigger stones. I pretended I was going to urinate and left the circle. As soon as I gained the nearest corner I began to run, stopping only when I had reached home. My wife was not there, so I stood by the window. Now that I was preparing to leave again, I noticed for the first time the trees in the garden beyond the wall. A breeze stirred them, and they swayed as if in the act of love. Our wall touched the next wall. The next wall nudged the next house with its shoulder, as if to pass on the news. Were I King Solomon, I would know what they were saying about the coming battle. I lowered my head. My head was like a flag at half-mast. Only then did I spy the slip of paper, left for me by my wife on the coffee table:

'I'm at mother's, come.'

I marvelled that the slip should be faded and yellow like a Dead Sea Scroll, for the note had been written only today and the paper had been white and fresh. Under the kites flown by the children, I skirted the city. In a nook where I had once made love, by the very rock, a sentry sat cooking himself a meal. He pointed at the kites in the sky and at the charred trunks of the olive trees. He pointed because his mouth was busy chewing. At his side lay a compass in which a needle nervously revolved. A boy ran after a dog which he held on a leash. What were they chasing, who chased them? A cannon stood in readiness beneath a latticework of thorns. I approached my mother's house from the valley, so that she had no advance warning. The road was inscribed with chalk arrows, all pointing in the same direction, as in a children's game. I practically followed them all the way. The quarter in which my mother lives is a small one, and is inhabited by artists and students and lofty trees and Yemenites and Germans and old settlers of Jerusalem who work in the foundations and the labour federation. Often when I am leaving the area on Saturday nights, I see crowds of people climbing the steps which lead into it. A young couple, pressed against each other; two girls, one pretty and the other with muscle-bound legs, returning from their youth centre. The neighbourhood swallows them all. A young man pushes a perambulator up the steps and his wife carries the baby. Dogs and cats. Even the letter-carrier who brings the mail. I have seen him only entering the neighbourhood, never leaving it – as if it refused to let him go. The same for the milkman, and another pair of lovers, who stroll side by side touching palms. Somebody is always playing the piano in my mother's neighbourhood. Sometimes the late sonatas of Beethoven, sometimes the early sonatas of first love. The neighbourhood swallows them all, and is never too full and never short of space. They never build new houses in it, or add new storeys to the old ones. Many of the apartments can be reached only by means of winding, open-air staircases. There is even a small public park, planted in honour of a soldier, a neighbourhood boy, who was killed. His father comes daily to water the trees. He leans over to water them with love, and the trees grow straight and their leaves are shiny. Sometimes the girl who plays the piano places a sprig of glossy eucalyptus leaves where her heart is. When her boy friend comes home from the army he kneads the leaves, and the pungent smell reaches his nose. The neighbourhood slopes towards the valley. Women set out their laundry and boys send up their kites, and all find their way to heaven.

I asked my mother for some sacks which might be filled with sand and used for protection against bombardment. My mother's attic is spacious, and full of old costumes for Purim masquerades. She took the pouch which held my father's prayer shawl, filled it with sand and sewed old clothes together into additional sacks – all because it was an emergency. I ate standing up. My wife was not there and came only at the last minute. She went with me to the assembly point. I noticed that the garden wall was caving in, that the well was empty and that the trenches by the roadside gaped as widely as ever. We walked through the narrow alleyways; it was afternoon and the streets were clear. A soldier stood on top of a high building, signalling with flags to a distant place. I signalled to myself inwardly, to my blood, which was sufficiently alarmed as it was. My sister stood in a telephone booth, placing a call. She could not let go of the receiver, but she gesticulated at me with her head. While her mouth talked into the distance, her eyes conversed with me. We have always had good times together, and now perhaps I am going to meet my death.

Battle for the Hill

When we were children we divided the world between us. Even when we were angry with each other and came to blows, we fought wisely and with a plan; I would turn my back to her and let her beat me with clenched fists without resisting. Then it would be my turn to beat her, and she would sit and not interfere. With that, the quarrel was over. Though we disagreed, we never enjoyed the blows, and our ears were insensitive to that wonderfully resonant drum, the pummelled body.

We reached the designated corner. My captain was waiting with some other members of the company. The truck was due in three minutes. My captain was angry because I had run away. He removed his eyeglasses, so as not to see the tears in the eyes of the women. I deposited the bag of candies on the ground; the paper was beginning to rip, and the coloured wrappers sparkled. The truck arrived, covered with drying mud. The motor started. 'It begins tonight,' whispered my captain into my ear. I knew that I would never see my wife again. It was a winter day, but her face was as dry as if it had been parched by a sirocco. She didn't want to cry but the tears came. Her whole body shared them, her hands and her legs, her hair and her thighs, until her torso became heavy and only her face remained dry. When we began to move it was like an eclipse of the moon. The side of the house encroached upon her fine, round face. Slowly the wall surged forward, until her face was completely covered. As she walked home she rocked back and forth a little. Her blood cried like an infant. She had to calm it. Her body was like a cradle for her blood, but the more she rocked it the harder it cried.

The truck jolted on and we rocked in it like drunkards. 'It's apparently scheduled for tonight,' said my captain, 'but I'm not entirely sure. We'll have to billet the company.' We found a house still in the process of construction. Part of it lay buried beneath wooden planks; the ceiling was dripping, for the concrete had only been poured the day before and a series of posts held it in place. We started to change our clothing: short pants for long, and long for short. The men scattered through the building. The rooms, which were not quite finished, rang with their voices. The practical jokers went about saying: This is the bathroom. This is the tub. I'm a gorgeous lady, soaping herself naked.

We sat upon sacks of cement near some barrels of white-wash, watching the patchy sky through blank windows. The night passed in a steady medley of men alighting from trucks and the clomp of boots, doors slamming and heavy utensils falling angrily. We lay in a small, empty room. The runner lay down at our feet. By his side were the machine gun, the ram's horn, and the evening paper. We were awakened frequently during the night by the arrival of reinforcements; shadowy men stood outside like beggars, waiting for us to find them a place and distribute arms. My captain got up in the middle of the night and left. When he returned, he proceeded to shine his flashlight on the sleeping men. He held a fresh packet of papers in his hand, like a bouquet – collections of orders. We got up and took our bearings anew; the enemy had strengthened the hill. There were cannon and minefields and women crying in village doorways. Some of the mines were exploding already, through mental telepathy. We were forced to revise the entire assault.

We crisscrossed the city, distributing ammunition. Everybody received a package. We hid ammunition in milk buckets, in toy boxes and underneath our hats, so that the enemy would not know where it was. In the morning, when we went to observe the hilltop, we saw that a change had come over it – like a body covered with freckles, it was arrayed with redoubts and fresh trenches. There were no shadows, and the wind piled the clouds in a high bank. I went to school. I meant to place a book upon the table, but instead I put down some bullets and an empty canteen. The children were wild and refused to settle down. The young teacher erased the board with her long hair and smiled at me. She was my substitute. I drew a plan of the hill on the blackboard with different coloured chalk. 'This is new territory,' I said. 'We will learn all about it.' I drew arrows, dotted lines, circles and crosses. The teacher laid her hand on my shoulder and said in a sad voice, 'Calm down, relax!' I erased the board and left. I ran all the way home; it was already evening, it was night. My wife was asleep; I didn't wake her. The world was quiet, and I lay on my back. The light from the neighbours' window cast an illuminated square upon the ceiling. People drifted home from their revelling. The young couple whose wedding picture I had seen somewhere in a photographer's box returned home too. The bride's voice was husky, sweet and honeyed in its lower register. Perhaps she sings too much at parties. Doors closed – of houses, of motorcars, of people. My eyes were wide open. Trucks passed, going in different directions. This reassured me. Had they been going in the same direction it would mean that the battle was starting; since they went in different directions, they meant no harm. I debated whether to wake my wife or let her sleep. Opportunities to talk are few. Always the stillness before the noise, and always the noise before the stillness. In the noise we cannot hear one another. In the stillness we cannot talk for fear of being overheard. I lay on my stomach, taking cover behind the pillow. In my mind's eye I saw the terrible hill. That very moment the area under barbed wire was being enlarged. An ocean of barbed wire. Half the company would be mowed down. I was about to doze off when there came a knock on the door. The front bell rang. The company clerk was pale: 'Come at once!' I dressed silently. The clerk had already gone ahead; he descended many steps, some of which weren't even there. My wife sat on the bed, hugging her knees close to her body, as if to say: these have remained loyal and stayed with me. I snatched a sweater from the chest of drawers. All the sweaters tumbled out, red ones and yellow ones, hers and mine. My wife sobbed like a child who has been roused from its sleep. I am going out to die. This time I said my good-byes to her forehead, rather than to her mouth or hand. Behind the hard forehead soft thoughts dwell, and beyond where thoughts harden, soft hair.

I went downstairs. I wanted to do it quietly, but my spiked boots shattered the silence. I headed for the unfinished building. Along the narrow walled pavement, a former pupil of mine knelt to fix her shoes. I asked her why she sat there after midnight. She looked me up and down, while her hands attended to the shoes.

'How was it on the kibbutz? Didn't you go to a kibbutz after finishing your studies?'

'It was lovely, but I've been left all alone. They've all gone off to the war, and my shoes have torn.'

I saw that she had grown up and would no longer listen to me. My pupils are scattered all over the world. One is already dead. I had no time to talk with the girl. She looked pretty in the beam of the flashlight. She squatted on one heel, fixing the shoe on the opposite foot. As she sat, her body seemed to fill out. Not so my thoughts, which were pointed like the prow of a ship. Why had she run away from home? I'm not going to war. The war is by my front step. The gate to my house is the beginning of the front. 'I don't understand you,' she said. 'When I was your pupil I never understood you either; then you used to scold me. Now I'm grown up and pretty, and I sit before you in the night between two walls and my thighs are full.'

A motorcyclist drove up, blinding me with his lights; he drew to a stop, and I hopped on to the back seat. The girl continued to squat on the pavement. Perhaps she saw an angel, blocking the road with drawn sword, someone I could not see. I came to the building; no one was there but the old watchman. The barrels of whitewash were where I had left them, as was the dripping from the concrete roof. A cat crossed between the watchman and me. 'They left an hour ago,' he said. 'See, the papers are still fluttering on the spot where company headquarters was. Here is a strap that was left behind.' I picked up a buckle from some piece of equipment. Where is my buckle, where does my life fasten? The buckle is death. It fits practically any strap. I threw the buckle away and wandered through the city, searching for my company. An engineering unit was throwing a temporary iron bridge across the square. I asked why they were building it but received no answer. A lone cannon rolled silently down the street on rubber wheels, until it ran into a telephone pole and came to a halt. An overturned car lay at the intersection, its wheels still spinning in the air. A pair of lovers came by and crawled into the cabin, sitting there upside-down while the wheels turned above them. I remembered a soldier in my unit who lived in an abandoned British army base. In order to get there I had to cut across an alleyway. 'So you've forgiven me, have you?' cried a voice from the cellar. Bending over, I caught sight of Nissim; myopic Nissim with the thick lenses, who was forever breaking his glasses and having to get a new pair made. He had never learned to fire a rifle, and we hadn't bothered to call him. He left the cellar, however, tagging along behind me until we reached the deserted base. Nothing was left of it but a couple of old stoves, a few ramshackle bungalows and an outhouse. Many things were scrawled on the walls of the outhouse: 'Out of bounds!' 'Officers only!' 'For children!' 'Auxiliary corps for women only!' Over these was written in Hebrew: 'Men.' 'Ladies.' 'Company D.' 'Yoska is an ass.' 'Down with German rearmament!' 'General John, go home!' 'For shame!' 'On with Spanish rearmament!'

I stood beneath the sign which said 'Out of bounds', but I was definitely within bounds. Bounded by death and by destiny. I saw the soldier I had been looking for sitting amongst some ruins, reading a book. His beard was short and fluffy, and he had a face like Jesus. When I seized him he said, 'I still haven't caught up on my sleep from the last mobilization. I need a great deal of sleep to nourish my thoughts.' I sent Nissim to have his glasses repaired because they broke. I was left with the soldier who resembled Jesus. The wire fence was like the crown of thorns placed around his head. A truck came by and we were handed a spool of telephone wires. The two of us grabbed a pole, and passing it through the cylinder we began to walk. There were many kinds of wire, in several colours. Wires for good news and for bad news, and wires for whispered longings, such as: Where are you?

I'm forbidden to say.
Raise your voice.
It's forbidden to raise it.
Raise your head.
It's raised.
I wish I could see you.
I'm like the receiver in your hands: ears to speak with and a mouth to listen.

We walked and walked until the wire ran out. We put down the empty metal spool. Children came and played with it, rolling it about. Girls jumped rope with the coloured wires. We passed on, treading on the chalk lines drawn by the children. The game the children play is not to step on the lines, but to jump over them. We stepped on them. God, or somebody like Him, does the same to us – as soon as we draw up rules and lines and boundaries, He comes with his monstrous feet and steps on them, because He doesn't care.

We came to a courtyard by the edge of the city which had an observation post. Every point in Jerusalem is a beachhead but everything is dry and there is no ocean of water. Yet the sea of Jerusalem is the most terrible sea of all. Every place in Jerusalem is a tongue of the city – and the city has many tongues and nobody understands her. I have tried many times to cut my ties with Jerusalem, and each time I have remained. If I come back safe and sound from the battle on the hill, I shall never return to Jerusalem!

I walked on, and as I walked I thought, a thinking

man walking along a street always looks beaten. A man walking in a khaki uniform is better off not thinking. One day they will arrest him and call him a traitor and demand to know his thoughts. My thoughts finally brought me to a narrow valley; my company was camped beneath the olive trees. I had not even had time to sit down before I was besieged with requests for passes. I had to give every man an answer, and no man was dispensable.

He said, 'I'm a storekeeper, the margarine is streaming through the cracks in the door.'

I answered, 'My longings for my wife are also streaming.'

He said, 'I haven't received my pay yet.'

I answered, 'Your children will collect your pay for you.'

He said, 'They won't give it to them without my signature.'

I answered, 'I have my signature and I still don't know who I am.'

He said, 'It's the anniversary of my father's death, I want to recite the mourner's prayer.'

I answered, 'We are all dying, and the clouds will rain upon us, and there's no need to pray.'

Hours passed, and I grew weary. Doctors and nurses came to examine our blood; a nurse jabbed her needle into a stray vein. A doctor saw the blood and said, 'It's no good.'

All the officers who were to take part in the attack gathered together. Artillery experts came to coordinate the shelling, chaplains to coordinate the aid of Providence, and every now and then somebody brought his wife. 'It's good for the women to see that it's not so terrible,' said our captain. Once more we attacked the hill and made calculations. Man and his guns preserve Thou, O Lord! Information arrived which put an entirely different slant on things: what we had thought to be barbed wire was really men, and what we had thought to be bunkers were gun emplacements. Once more nothing was certain. Death alone was certain for all. I revised the map according to the latest information.

My ink ran out. I borrowed a pen from my wife. The pen fell between the ammunition crates, on which was written: 'Fragile, Handle with Care', 'No Smoking, Explosive Material', 'Keep In a Cool Dark Place.' I too wanted to lie down in a cool dark place, and write 'Handle With Care' on myself. I never found the pen, but the panic I experienced on the first night failed to return. Sometimes a great clarity strikes me flush between the eyes. Autumn days come, cleansing the troubled winds of summer. A group of soldiers crouched by a dip in the valley and played at Questions and Answers. I knew that on the following evening they would be asking no questions, but would be lying in wait for the zero hour. Among a patrol of riflemen I met my little pupil Mazal, who is seven years old. She has large eyes, her mother is a slut and her father is an Arak drinker. 'I'm going off to the war with you,' she said. 'I'm a nurse, and I have a white cap and a white apron left over from Purim.'

'You have to go home. Your mother will worry.'

'She won't worry.'

'And your little brothers?'

'I've already taken care of them and fixed them some food.'

'It's not Purim now. You have to go to school.'

'They don't let me go because I have lice in my hair. The teacher made me leave.'

'Rinse your hair with kerosene and have it cut!'

She shook her black curls. 'I won't cut it, I'm going to war with you. If I cut it I won't be strong. Didn't we learn about Samson?'

'But a little girl like you has to keep clean,' I told her.

She threw me a long look which travelled from one end of Jerusalem to the other. I sat her down in the playground which had been converted into the evacuation centre for the wounded. She started to play with the dolls. She listened to their heartbeat and gave them injections. One of the dolls was exuding dry seaweed and she bandaged it. Chairs scraped overhead; I could tell that the staff meeting was over. I heard men jumping into trucks, the clank of metal, and meters turning over. My captain came in and saw Mazal, but said nothing; he waved the bundle of papers in his hand. I grabbed hold of Mazal and we climbed together to the attic. We could see the hill. 'Your eyes are tired,' she said, 'let me look.' I gave her the binoculars.

'What do you see, Mazal?'

'Men standing and passing green crates.'

'What else?'

'Many sacks, and barbed wire like a lot of curls.'

'What else?'

'Now they're hiding. All I see is bushes and mounds of dirt.'

I came down with Mazal from the observation post and asked my wife to take her home. They linked hands and disappeared. Everything is always disappearing, and I can retain nothing. 'Where is the young girl?' I asked the tenants, 'the one who sings in the bathtub?' She had gone to a party for the American marines who work at the Consulate. I stood in the doorway. Tracers lit the night, but the eternal light within my brain flickered silently and feebly. I went to the American building. A row of coloured bottles stood against the wall. I watched the girl dance; her crinolines flapped about her waist, a red crinoline and a black one and a white one. She didn't notice me. She only stopped dancing when her thighs grew chilly. The American marines laughed, and she joined in their laughter. The American flag rippled like waves. I stepped outside. I passed a hard wall. I wanted to press myself against the terrible wall of history, like Rashi's mother.* I wanted to find myself a niche safe from an intransigent History. I

*According to an old Jewish legend, the mother of Rashi, the famous eleventh-century Biblical exegete, was walking one day in a narrow, walled-in street in Worms during her pregnancy. A carriage came towards her and she was in danger of being crushed; she pressed herself against the wall behind, and the wall miraculously opened to receive her.

wanted a miracle to come to pass, so I should not have to lie
mutilated on the hillside.

I returned to my pup-tent. I thought a lot. I heard a
voice saying, 'At exactly eleven-fifty-eight we begin the
bombardment.' I thought some more. Finally, I raised
my hand and switched off my thoughts the way you switch
off a bed lamp. I was awakened frequently during the
night. I imagined I was being called. I fell asleep again. A
cold wind blew through the valley, slicing it open like a
knife gutting fish. In the morning I couldn't tell whether
there had been an attack or not. We continued to observe
the hill. The earth was like those Christian saints who suffer
from stigmata on their hands and feet, where the nails
passed through Jesus and the cross. The earth was like
them, bursting open where the shells were due to fall.

We strengthened our positions. We filled sandbags, and
went off with our girl friends and wives to make love. We
strolled down the streets, singing and dancing. One day a
soldier approached me and I asked him what unit he belonged to. 'I have no unit,' he answered. 'What is that
insignia on your shoulder?' 'It's not an insignia. It's a
patch. My shirt ripped.' I noticed that some of his front
teeth were missing. The company runner appeared, and I
recalled that it was my job to see about hot drinks. I re-
quisitioned a number of soldiers and we set off with empty
buckets in our hands. We went to the large kitchen in the
basement. It was not yet daybreak. Shouting to make themselves heard, the cooks moved among the lurid flames as if
they were in Hell. 'Where is the tea?' I shouted. The head
cook pointed to a bucket. An oily, metallic, vaporous smell
filled the air. We passed through the small courtyard, skid-
ding on our boots. A fine rain began to fall. From the
communications office came the laughter of the women
operators. We put down our buckets and peered through
the lighted windows. Even then the tea refused to calm
down. All we saw in the window was the light.

That whole day the men practised rapid mobilization.

Battle for the Hill

First they were told to go to work, and they went. Then the alarm was sounded, and they were made to lie in the trenches, in readiness for the attack. By evening we had reached a terrific speed of mobilization – the men threw away their work tools on the double and were handed rifles. In this manner I managed to spend part of my time in school. I appeared suddenly from behind a map of Asia Minor, frightening the children. My captain came in the night: Now it's in earnest! I looked him in the eyes.

'You're joking.'

'No, this time it's serious.'

The men were already asleep in their jumping-off positions. We went to take a last look. The streets were empty, and the vacant lots were hoarse as if from too much shouting. We lay down in a briar patch opposite the hill. My captain and I dozed off from time to time. In the early hours of the morning I suddenly asked, 'How much longer?' He shook his head, and the bushes rustled by his shoulder. At daybreak I noticed that the bush above my head was larger than my head, and larger than the rising sun. I noticed that the dry grass beside me swayed and trembled, while the grass in the distance was tranquil. The world resembles men who are all looking around a corner at the same thing. I watch them from a distance, and cannot tell what it is they find so fascinating. We went to sit at a marble table in a small restaurant and made a complete inventory: the delivery of weapons after the hill was taken and the evacuation of the wounded. We heard the clanking of metal. My captain jumped to his feet and shouted, 'The tanks are coming!' We saw there were no tanks, only a truck piled high with bottles. We laughed. Rather than look at the enemy hill, I looked towards the city. I saw men walking about and children playing, and I could not go back. Towards evening my men began to abandon their positions one by one, slipping away to their homes. I tried to stop them. 'Let them go,' said my captain. 'Soon they will come back anyway.' I took my wife by the hand, and as we walked I told her about the hill. Every Saturday we go to look at it. Now and then I see my captain. Once, while sitting in the barber's chair to have my hair cut, I glanced in the mirror and saw my captain passing in the street. Sometimes my whole life passes before my eyes in the barber's mirror. I jumped from the chair. I paid for my haircut, and rushed out to the street to run after him. My captain was already gone.

Yehuda Amichai

Nina of Ashkelon

Translated by
Ada Hameirit-Sarell

Once I had a summer girl who left me at summer's end. At first I thought when she left and autumn came that if she hadn't gone there would have been no autumn, that her leaving had caused the coming of autumn. Since then I have learned that there was no connection between the two events. There are many such parallel cycles: the cycle of seasons, the cycle of my life, the cycle of my loves, and that of my loneliness. Because of her and others too, and because of all of these, I was late going on my vacation to Ashkelon.

I came to the place like the Roman merchant who was buried there upon his return from a visit to Southern Italy, his birthplace; he returned to the East and died. Artists were brought to decorate the interior of his grave. This same Roman merchant inspired various reflections and dreams in me. Not far from the hotel was his grave, in a hollow between two sand dunes.

People sitting on the grass in the hotel garden said: 'One has to see the antiquities.' Why are people in our country so excited about antiquities? Perhaps because the present is not certain, and the future less so. In ancient times they used to forecast the future. Now we programme the past.

In the evening, the proprietor of the hotel strolled among his guests, delighted to see that they ate with gusto. He was red all over, like sausages boiled in water. Sometimes he put his hands on the table as if he wanted to serve himself up, so eager was he to please his guests. Aside from myself, the guests included a young couple who had been married the day before, and a muscular German woman with a strong, aggressive voice, and many others.

The next day we went to the historic excavations near the hotel. In the grave of the Roman merchant were some mosaics and broken pillars and marking places for the archaeologists — little notations like price tags in a shop window. Also there were chalk lines and wires strung about to aid the digging. We clustered around our guide. Once upon a time I hated to go to such places in an organized group. Now I loved the crowd, the closeness of bodies, the voices. Watch your step, behold, see the bas relief. Marvellous!

Sometimes I return alone to a place like this after having toured it with a group. And so it happened that in the evening I returned to the dead Roman's grave and sat in the soft, loose sand among the slips of paper and wires. On the road a car was passing slowly, like a police car, cruising, looking for something. Young men and women were sitting in the car, discussing whether they should stop and get out. Finally they drove on towards the tall tower in town. I studied the excavations. As in an architect's plan, you could see the foundations. This was house construction in reverse. The site had been turned into a plan, the plan flew into the builder's head, and from his head to the wide world.

I walked down to the sea and took off my shoes. The small crabs fled from me and disappeared into their holes, as did the sun, which was speeding towards the hole in the West where it would vanish. I watched the sun set while tying my sandals. We have learned to perform many actions simultaneously: I could sit tying on my sandals, sit and kneel and look towards the setting sun. If we are trained well, we can do three or four things together at the same time: ride in a car, cry, and look through a window; eat, love, think. And all the time consciousness passes like an elevator among the floors.

Later in the evening, a movie was shown in the garden.

Everyone took a chair and sat down. Dogs and children ran about, draining off the attention of the audience; then they ran away and our attention returned to the preparations for the movie, the memory of supper, and gossip. The movie projectionists arrived late. A chair was placed on top of another chair to raise the projector to the proper height. The movie was about dancing, stabbing, and loving, all three of which seemed to be going on at the same time.

A girl passed between the screen and the projector. All the adventures mounted her back. I was jealous of her; she smiled. Her body moved in her dress as in a sea. Tomorrow she would go down once more to the soft beach. She did not have to labour much; life came her way, as readily as the movie that was now being shown on her white back. Two dogs jumped on each other. In a distant wing of the hotel a light went on. Someone left the audience. Someone didn't feel well. From the kitchen we heard the voice of a girl, singing.

The hotel owner said, 'Later we shall go down to the beach and fry sausages.' Those were his exact words. The movie ended and the chairs were left for the waiters to replace. We all descended to the beach. On the way we passed Shemuel's coffee-house, where there were many pillars and a paved floor for dancing. That was Shemuel's coffee-house. Shemuel had tried many things before he opened his coffee-house near the sea that was black by night and green by day. That evening he had strung coloured bulbs in happy chains in the sky of his coffee-house, along the tops of the pillars which surrounded the dance floor. He governed his skies with the help of electric wires at night, and by day with canvas awnings that fenced out the noonday sun. That evening, soldiers from a near-by camp sat under his skies near the whispery sand. They had come to celebrate a victory, or to be comforted after defeat. At any rate, they had come to rest from the training-grounds, the outposts, and the army offices. Silken girls put fumbling hands on their shoulders. Girls with rosy ice-cream thighs and eyes of chocolate cake. Whispering sand-girls who kept their warmth at night. Some of the soldiers had come with their heavy boots on, and danced like bears, swayed like drunkards. Shemuel looked upon all of them with pleasure and satisfaction; every once in a while he took a tray and passed among the dancers to attend to their wishes. We decided to postpone the sausage business until the following night. Some of the older women wanted to stay and watch the young soldiers dance. We sat with the local doctor. He nudged my shoulder and said: 'Look, there is Shemuel's beautiful wife.'

She was standing near the exit, in front of a sign which said: 'Discount for soldiers. Today – shashlik and liver.' She had green eyes and a week ago she had returned to her husband. Once, a rich American had come to Ashkelon and she had run after him – literally. They had exchanged a few words while she served him in her husband's restaurant, then, simple as it sounds, she ran to the kitchen, threw off her apron, and ran after him across the sands through the thin bushes. That is to say, sitting in his hotel room in the town of Ashkelon, he did not yet know that she was pursuing him. Her shoes had filled with sand and she threw them away, she almost did the same with her skirt and lace panties. All these things – shoes, clothes, strange thoughts, the outgrowths of culture – disturbed her in her flight and her green eyes were those of a wildcat in an ancient forest. It was early morning when she arrived at the American's room. The next day she married him and they left together. After three months she returned. It is not to be supposed that she crossed the sea on her own power, although she was an able swimmer and fully capable of leaving her clothes in a heap near the shore in Naples and swimming to the shores of Israel. How and why they parted was not known.

Anyway, she came back through the sands, without a suitcase and clad in the same dress she had been wearing when she left; she was tired and barefoot. A week ago the exact same thing happened; she came back, dishevelled, from a similar adventure, and refused to utter a word. She had to be taught to speak all over again.

That evening, as I have said, she stood near the exit, framed by the large sign, green-eyed, nose tossing, her mouth large and quiet in her white, traveller's face. The fat doctor looked her over and said: 'She is ready for new sands and new dances. That one will never be cured. She's like a Siamese twin to the whole world. A new American will come, or even a Greek or a Roman, as they used to come here in ancient days, and she will run after him.' The doctor pointed to the Roman's tomb and fell silent.

One of the officers on the dance floor went out, picked some narcissus flowers, and handed them to her. She said to him: 'I know their scent.' He answered: 'I do not yet know yours.' She said: 'For you it is not worthwhile.' Her husband was not jealous, and he permitted the officer to hand her the flowers. Shemuel had learned not to be jealous. Every day he wrote out the menu on the board in front of which his wife was now standing. He knew what was to be served at the noon meal, and he knew whether there would be a dance for the soldiers in the evening. But he didn't know if his wife would stay with him.

A dog ran after a moth but failed to trap it. A soldier caught his girl while dancing and lifted her up, swung her about like a young palm branch so that she would bring him a blessing. Shemuel's wife stood still, as if she were examining cloth in a shop. Her eyes were open. The moth tried to fly into her eyes; she shut her lids. The elderly guests returned to the hotel. The doctor stayed with us. The soldiers returned to camp. No one blew the bugle.

At breakfast, conversation was lively. Plans for the day were spread out on the tables. Most of the women came down in shorts; the older the woman, the shorter the shorts. After the meal I strolled out towards the bushes, to the site of ancient Ashkelon. I had seen the area by night, surrounded and protected from the three winds by a rampart on which could be seen the remains of walls and towers, and in the West the sea. At night it had looked foreboding and sombre, like a snarled entanglement with no exit. So I had decided to explore the area by morning light.

Still, the moment I entered the tangled bushes, my mood became blunt and heavy; I felt threatened. After walking a few hundred yards down the blue road, I reached the edge of the ancient town-site. My feet sank into the flour-like sand. Instantly I found myself in a deserted orange grove. In our country we are used to deserted places, to seeing houses without roofs, windows without houses, bodies without life, blackened plantations, and the remains of cracked roads. But nothing ever nauseated me as much as that orange grove. The dead branches were covered with white snails, the whole grove seemed stricken with leprosy. I stared at the broken aqueducts, partly filled by sand from the sea. Thorns at once beautiful and terrible twined their way to the tops of the branches. There were dark corners among the trees that were too large, too large for their own good: ruined corners that guarded the sterility of their shadows. Green flies buzzed around the sweat on my forehead. I continued walking. Fat fruits dropped from sycamore trees and burst on the ground. Everywhere there was the depressing sensation of sand over dead bodies, of dead bodies over the earth. Sand flies burst in a cloud. The road turned, pathways opened, leading into thickets of tamarisks, pathways at the end of which anything at all might happen. A lair of dark curses in various Mediterranean tongues, the vomit of cultures torn from their homeland and transported here. Now this unholy thicket had all those layers beneath it. Such Mediterranean trickery! Phoenician merchants, Greek merchants, Jewish merchants – striking bargains with heaven and with the dead, bringing the smell of perfume and expensive cloth to the detriment of the native population. It is like this: a skeleton, but not yet a clean skeleton; the odour of a rotting cadaver. I do not mean the odour of the coyotes and wildcats that die night after night in this thicket among the salted branches covered with snails. Such an odour would not nauseate me as did the sweet smell of this skeleton, but not yet a skeleton, of the ancient cultures rotting here in this thicket.

Here, for example, is a sycamore tree, leaning sideways in an unnatural fashion. I know there are trees near the sea and on the slopes that have been bent by the wind, but these sycamores had been permanently twisted by some intrinsic, predetermined corruptness. This landscape had been prostituted, pampered, spoiled. It destroyed its stomach on sweets. It should not pretend now to have a face of white marble, a girl's face, the tanned face of a soldier. All that is conjuring.

But I, at least, knew what lay underneath, what nourished the sycamores and the groves, what had really caused the marble pillars to be built. Even those narcissus flowers, so innocent in their whiteness – where did they get that exaggerated scent? It did not come from the sand. Indeed, it is best not to inquire what is in their roots. And those flies of Beelzebub that prey on live bodies and sculptures alike? I speak here of things which have refused to die, that continue an underground existence, beneath the sand and beneath the water, like submerged and incoherent whispers. A landscape that tosses in its bed with wild dreams. And what about that figure of Pan in the Roman's grave? By what metamorphosis did it arrive on this shore? And Shemuel's wife – where was she from? How did she escape, running through the sands, through the sea? And her green eyes?

I went on until I reached the small amphitheatre where statues and broken mosaic tiles and Greek ledges lay about in disorder. Every historical period had collected in this hole, as in a textbook. The wind rose from the sea and the trees leaned towards the East.

From the amphitheatre I took a side trail and walked down past one of the terrible sycamores that bent almost to the earth – that is to say, it was still standing, but in repose. The sycamore was not dead, because the ends of its branches sprouted leaves and sickening, fat fruits. An old, crumbling well-house stood there, with an apparatus made of a double chain and small rectangular scoops for drawing water. I did what every man does when he passes a well: I threw a stone into it, but I heard nothing, neither the sound of water nor the smack of stone on stone. I threw a second stone, but nothing happened. I tried to pull the draw chain. I bent over and suddenly I felt myself covered with a cold sweat. I turned around.

Shemuel's wife was sitting on the trunk of the sycamore, swinging. She bared her teeth:

'Such a one as you are then, a snooper.'

'Where do you know me from?'

'You – don't you live in the hotel?'

'Yes . . . but you . . .'

'Yesterday you were sitting with the fat doctor. He is also my doctor. How funny he is. When he examined me after I came back he wanted to kiss me. He's the same size as the Roman merchant buried in the sands.'

'What do you know about the merchant?'

'And what are you looking for underneath this town?'

'I'm not looking for anything.'

All that time she was sitting swinging on that evil tree. Then she asked me:

'Have you been to the ancient harbour already?'

Again she bared her teeth, then jumped off the tree in a bound and disappeared down one of the trails, parting the bushes with her hands to work her way through. The bushes sprang back after she passed. I was still standing near the old well. Nothing had changed here, I saw. This landscape was no more strange and terrible today than it was a week ago, years ago, millennia ago. Shemuel's wife could as easily have sat in the private amphitheatre watching two wrestlers as she stood last night on the dance floor, watching the soldiers. I can imagine one of the wrestlers felling his opponent, then kneeling over him, gripping him with tong-like thighs while looking up at her for further instructions. She sticks to character: 'Continue to the death!' The results are known. One of the two, the one lying upon the ground, grapples the other's chest with such force that a jet of blood breaks from his nostrils. The results are well known, known to this landscape, to the sycamore, to the marble, and to the wife of Shemuel, who pretends.

I went on to the harbour and stood on the hill where the pillars faced the sea and there were no ships. In the distance I saw the beach. A whitened skeleton of a cat lay in the deep grass. Near it was a yellow paper and empty cans. I saw that I was standing above some Arab houses. Suddenly I heard a voice calling me; it was the masculine woman from the hotel. All this time I had tried to avoid her, but now I was happy to see her waving to me from the trail. At once the spell vanished. Together we climbed the sand ramparts above which stood the remnants of an ancient wall. She said: 'I saw Shemuel's wife, the one from last night. She's a whore. Do you like her?' As she said this she poked me in the chest with her fist and laughed in a coarse, masculine manner. 'When I was young, the men looked for sporty girls. I was good at winter sports. I caught my husband on a steep slope in the Alps. What do young men look for today? Fluttering, spoiled, green-eyed elastic-limbed females like Shemuel's wife.'

In the midst of this one-sided conversation we reached the orange groves at the entrance to the ancient town. I discovered that many of the trees bore green fruit. It was the end of summer and yet the fruit had not ripened. On a single, broken branch, two oranges were yellowing in sterile, premature ripeness.

Before arriving at the hotel I took leave of my sportive companion, and was again rewarded with a punch that shook me to my bones. I went down to the sea. This time the beach was empty. I had not realized that I had spent almost a whole day on the site of ancient Ashkelon. A blackbird perched on a pillar that had once been consecrated to the gods. Two girls rolled in the sand and shouted. The sea left lines in the sand, but it was impossible to read the future in the palm of this shore. I ran after a crab that was sparkling with a strange silver colour, but the silver – a tiny fish, the crab's prey – disappeared. The tamarisks finished their preparations for the night. The sun began to descend into the sea. When I returned to the hotel I was once more surprised by the amount of time that had passed.

After supper, the red-faced hotel keeper donned a white hat and apron. With a huge fork in his hand, he entered the reading room: 'Be ready to go down to the sea.' Two cooks were kept busy transporting a large stove to the beach; one of the young hotel maids adorned her neck with chains of red sausages, the way daughters of the Hawaiian Islands decorate themselves with flower chains. A merry procession then made its way to the sands. The young married couple preferred not to join us, but remained seated in the reading room. They had not yet acquired an apartment, and they wanted to make believe they owned the hotel.

The landlord and the masculine woman did most of the talking. It did their hearts good to be on the beach, so they began singing, first a Hebrew song, then German hiking songs. The landlord's white hat served to illuminate the way for us. The sea was lazy that night and the moon had not yet come up. The cooks placed the stove on the sand and began stoking it with charcoal. Everyone was enchanted with the blaze, especially those who were close to the stove. Behind us dozed the sombre mass of ancient Ashkelon. I did not sit close to the fire. We finished eating the sausages. Then came water-melon, and after the water-melon there were party games. One or two people would leave the group, the rest sat around in a circle, whispering. Then the people who left were called back; they were supposed to guess the plans of those who were sitting in the circle. Later, someone brought out a drum and a harmonica and everyone became sad. Still later they started dancing.

'Let's dance barefoot!' The hotel owner began to worry about the good name of his hotel, and about the welfare of the stove. He told the cooks to take the stove back to the hotel. Some people came from Shemuel's café – a few officers, some girl soldiers, the doctor and his quiet wife, and also Shemuel and his wife. At first they participated in the dancing and singing, then they split into separate groups. Suddenly, Shemuel's wife got up and ran in the direction of the waves. She left her shoes near me. The doctor said: 'It is nothing. That is always her custom. It is a sort of courtesy visit she pays to the sea.'

After a few minutes she came back, all wild and untidy and strange, the hems of her dress wet like lips after drinking. She caught up the hem of her dress and squeezed water out of it and bared her teeth in my face like a terrible biting animal. I saw that her watch was wet. She took it off and held it between her teeth.

I told her: 'Your watch got wet.'

She took her watch out of her mouth and put it next to my ear. Then she walked away. From walking she switched to jumping and from jumping to high, wonderful dance steps near the sea. When she returned, she said to me, 'This is a *mitzvah* dance.'

I said: 'What's possessed you, Penina?'

She laughed and said: 'My name is not Penina. They call me Nina.'

'A nice name that is.'

'That isn't the entire name. They call me Nina the Seagull.'

Her voice was hoarse, as if lined with salt and seaweed. Shemuel approached and said:

'Here is a crate brought here by the sea. Once the sea brought a crate full of sardines. Once it brought a young dead whale. The sea brings many strange things. It brings things to my wife too. Sometimes in the morning I see strange objects lying near her sleeping body, like branches, like snails, like objects from an ancient ship that foundered on the rocks. Maybe you could tell me what to do about her?'

'Get her pregnant.'

Shemuel laughed, and sighed, and then became silent. Later, one of the officers suggested playing tag near the sea. I remained sitting with Shemuel, who was slow. The doctor took part in the game, then he joined us. Because of his fat belly he couldn't keep running very long. Shemuel stopped talking when the doctor approached. Suddenly we heard screams and laughter and before I knew what had happened Nina jumped up and hid behind me. A young officer passed by us, running in great strides; he didn't realize that she was hiding. Nina's heart was beating hard.

The moon began to rise. Everybody put on bathing suits and went into the sea. Nina's voice was hoarse. All that she had left behind in the world was her little bundle of clothes on the wide sands. The doctor said: 'After all, God himself is like that. He is far away from us, and all He left behind is a little pack of clothes on the vast sand, and to us that seems God.' Nina screamed from the sea. I rose in alarm, but the doctor calmed me: 'That is her custom. Don't be alarmed.' I left the doctor and Shemuel and God and Nina's parcel of clothes and joined another group. The masculine woman was among them, demonstrating such heroic feats as running fast, lifting rocks, and other manly deeds. The soldiers stood around her. Some tried to race with her, but she always won. When I approached she shouted: 'Come, come!'

Afterwards they brought drinks and we drank and the night never became cold. They made a fire in the sand out of old crates. I heard a whisper, a moan: 'Get me out! Get me out!' Nobody heard it but me. I went in the direction of the voice. Nina was buried up to her hips in the sand, like a statue found on the beach, laughing. I uncovered her.

'Why don't you ask me? Sometimes intelligent people

and artists come from the city and they are glad to find an interesting type like me.'

'If I asked, you would lie to me anyway.'

'But that, too, is a truth.'

'I was convinced you had a fish-tail like the daughters of the sea.'

'Come with me to the hotel bar,' Nina said.

I agreed; we went up to the hotel in our bathing suits. In came the suntanned Roman merchant and sat with us at the bar. There was no bartender because the hour was late. I went behind the bar and served them. The Roman looked in my direction and said: 'Who is he?'

Nina said: 'He's mine. I caught him in the sea.'

The merchant looked at me from under his short, curly hair and said: 'He is good for the big games in the arena.' They both laughed until I fell asleep.

I woke up as the first morning chill penetrated the room. I heard a car stop; a man jumped out and called for the café owner. I came out wearing pyjamas. The man seemed to have come from afar; he asked me: 'Are you the café owner?' I explained that I was not the café owner and that this was a hotel. I could not see clearly in the early dawn.

He said: 'Never mind. Come quick!'

I climbed into his car and we drove the length of the shore road in the direction of the dunes. He stopped the car in the high grass, jumped out and ran towards the sea. A woman was lying under a rough army blanket. I was alarmed.

'Don't be afraid,' my companion said. Angrily, he pulled the blanket from the figure. The woman was nude. She woke up instantly. It was Nina.

'What are you doing here?' I asked.

'Are you a worrier too? Enough people worry about me.'

I told her: 'Come back with me to your home.'

She laughed: 'I have no clothes. He took my clothes as a pawn.'

I advised her to cover herself with the blanket. The man who drove me out said: 'The blanket is mine. I was passing by and saw a woman lying nude on the sand by the first light of dawn, and I covered her.' Finally he agreed to drive us home. On the way she cried on my shoulder.

Shemuel was waiting at the gate of his house. All that day Nina didn't show up at the beach. I sat in the sand by myself and felt the first winds of autumn. Many of the awnings that had been spread against the summer sun were now torn. Papers were flying about or lay on the beach, covered with sand. A group of soldiers, boys and girls, arranged themselves to be photographed, then rearranged themselves after each snapshot. The ones who were standing lay down, a boy put his hand on a girl's shoulder, they posed in profile, then in groups of two and five, and then they all lay down as if dead. The two girls I had seen earlier rolling in the sand came over. They were still laughing and rolling. One of them wore a red bathing suit and her face was loud with pleasure. Everyone cleared a passage for them and they rolled on by us. The place where we had sat the night before was already covered with new sand. The old people sat in red lounge chairs and looked at the sea and waited in silence for death – hoping that death, too, would come to them in silence. Where do they derive their certainty that death will come from the West?

Near the lifeguard's tower a crowd had gathered. Two women undressed underneath a towel, twisting like snakes so as not to reveal their bodies. The lifeguard's skin was covered with tattoos and drawings of daughters of the sea, flowers, and an anchor in deep grass. People dragged up lounge chairs. A woman came out dressed in a white apron embroidered with the Star of David. She turned to me: 'Do you see that blanket? The grey one?'

'Yes, I see it.'

'Yesterday it was used to cover a dead man who had drowned.'

A girl walked by, arm-in-arm with a young man. The

camera hanging on his bare chest was like a third eye. They chatted together, then the girl began to leap in happy dancing steps. She ran up to a sandstone boulder, leaned against it with her hands folded behind her back, her face to the sea. There she stood like Andromeda in the Greek legend, waiting for her saviour. She wore a helpless smile. The lifeguard, big and husky, walked towards her with a camera in his hands. She stood against the rock; there was no place for her to hide. He came closer, raised a hand as if to hold up a sword, counted aloud, one, two, three, and the girl, saved, jumped against him. But he was too busy turning knobs keeping the pictures in order.

Later, the afternoon games began. Mothers called their children. All the gods in heaven and on earth called their prophets, who began to prophesy without pity, near the terrible woods and the sea. Towards nightfall, everything awoke, and the foreign sea gurgled in small waves towards the beach. People shook the sand from their bodies as if preparing for the resurrection. Some of them walked over to the concrete breakwater where they sat emptying the sand from their sandals and stockings and hair. They were all in a hurry to forget the sea. The shoreline, too, was in a hurry, and raced to join the sea and the sandstone wall at the horizon. I knew it was a false joining, a play of perspective. Everything was an illusion of the eyes. The children's cries, too, joined the great silence on the horizon. And everything covered itself with the sombre soft grass of night. The sea's thoughts were dry and empty like darkening ears of corn thrown on to the sand. Everything was burnt.

I lay for a short while longer in the sand, watching the feet of those returning home. Then I too returned to the hotel, where I saw Nina sitting on the terrace. Her limbs were elastic and brown from a surfeit of sun. She was wearing red shorts that were so tight I could see the crease of her buttocks. I sat next to her, behind a bush that had provided a screen for us. She rested her feet on the railing, lifting her legs until they looked like a gate, like wings. Then she laughed: 'This morning you were quite alarmed – this morning when he awakened you and you found me lying among the weeds at dawn.'

We watched a procession of black ants traverse the terrace floor. Nina put on her glasses and took a letter out of her purse. I asked if it was from an admirer. She said she had no admirer because one did not admire her but became crazy about her. Did it please her to have men become crazed at the sight of her face? Why not? Why, then, did she, too, become crazed when she lay out on the sands covered by a strange blanket? She was infected by the craziness of the crazed. There was nothing left for me to say to her. Nina took out her hairpins, letting her hair fall. Her hair flowed down to her waist, to her hips. And my thoughts at that instant were unknit and wild.

In the evening I took leave of Shemuel, her good husband. The next day I was to return to my town. Shemuel received me by himself. We talked about all the subjects in the world but Nina. Each time we felt the conversation coming around to Nina I led him around the subject without fail. Later, I got up to say good-bye. The bedroom door was open and I saw Nina lying in bed. One of her eyes was hidden by the pillow. The second was awake and open. For me, it will never close.

The next day I returned home and right away started work and forgot everything. My profession is to forget; my destination is to remember. One evening I forgot to shut off the radio after the news broadcast. I went to shut it off when they began to announce that the Israeli police were asking for the public's help to locate a certain Nina. They mentioned her family name. Last seen wearing a striped white skirt and a white blouse with rolled sleeves. I returned to my guests and remained silent. How had I seen her last? Dressed in short red pants and with her hair loose. We sat up until midnight and talked about the announcements that are made to the public concerning missing persons. One of my guests said that it was all exaggerated. No sooner does someone go to visit his friends than everybody gets alarmed and announces on the radio that he is lost. Many people get lost in the world. Some of them are announced, some not. I told my guests that in Nina's case it was very serious and that I knew her. At midnight I suddenly heard voices coming from one of the houses near by. A woman was screaming through her tears: 'Go away! Leave me alone, you bastard!' I stood near the window. I saw nothing and then the voices stopped. A train whistled as it passed through the valley. It seemed to me that I had heard Nina's voice. Maybe she needed help. Maybe she was hiding in one of the houses in the neighbourhood. The suntanned Roman, who once sat with us at the bar, must have kidnapped her. Maybe they were still hiding around Ashkelon, in the white sands, among the statues.

The following day there was another call for help on the radio. But in this broadcast Nina was described as wearing red pants and with her hair wild. They also announced the languages she knew, and some of the special habits she had, like pulling up her knees, and such personal characteristics as the smile in her eyes. I remembered her with one eye hidden in the pillow and one eye awake and staring. Poor Nina – she must certainly be very tired, wandering through the world with a Roman who wore the uniform of a UN officer. I was sure that he would treat her rudely whenever she became tired or asked for a few minutes' rest by the side of the blue road.

And so the two of them wandered about, hiding from time to time in various places. Once they hid at the house of her girlfriend, who was an expert manicurist. In the same building there was a movie theatre, and her friend's apartment adjoined the projection booth and loudspeakers. The soundtrack could be heard on the staircase. I came in haste but Nina was not there. Her friend asked me if I wanted a manicure.

Then they hid in the Caves of the Judges in Sanhedria.

Nina sat, her head leaning on his chest; she was pulling and tearing at the hair on his bare chest. Near them was a radio in a small suitcase. To the police description of Nina the Roman added his own: her breasts are brown and small, her thighs are fast and never rest.

On the next news bulletin they again detailed the languages Nina knew. All the Mediterranean tongues: a little bit of Greek and a little Italian and Spanish and Hebrew and a bit of Arabic.

One night, walking along the street, I saw a display window that was still lit. It belonged to a dress shop. One of the big mannequins in the window moved and I saw that it was Nina. Quickly she came out to me and said, 'Be quiet, be quiet, don't say a thing.' Also, she said that it had become impossible for her to imagine his hands without his voice, nor his eyes without his blood, and at last she said: 'I am happy in my wanderings. Don't reveal anything to anyone, otherwise I will die.'

I told her: 'All this will end in a terrible fall, like the fall of the sycamore fruits.'

They began to change their clothing from time to time to avoid being recognized. The radio description no longer corresponded to the real Nina. Yet, if they had known her true description and had searched with true love they would have found them easily. After a while the broadcasts stopped and the police began looking for other people: lunatics who had escaped from asylums, children who had run away from home. One evening, as I was on my way home, I was reminded of a letter that had been lying in my inside pocket. In the street the children were throwing stones at the metal telephone poles, and the poles rang out with each hit. Sometimes a little piece of paper in your pocket becomes more important than all the stones and metal and houses in the outside world. I opened the letter and knew where they were. They had reached the ruined crusader's castle that is near Jerusalem and is called Aqua Bella.

I went there alone. Near the road lay the charred trunk of an olive tree, and near the tree grew five red poppies. I reached the fountains near the ruin. The two of them were sitting under a tall oak tree. Their sandals lay near by and their belts were loose — a sign that they intended to remain here for a while. I looked into their eyes with an inquisitorial gaze. First I spoke to him alone near one of the thick roots, but he didn't listen to me. His hair was smooth and had been greased with shiny oil. My words did not stay with him. Nina's hair was loose; dry oak leaves and flying thorn seeds clung to it. Her hair was open, and my words clung to her heart. I sat opposite her in the arch of the ruined window over the fountain. Nina didn't look too happy. Vagabonding was not good for her. Her eyes were too wide. She had not slept. Questions and replies played about her eyes and mouth and ears and in her anxious sleep; there were few answers in her mouth. The night came and devoured us like the wolf in the fairy tale.

The next day Nina returned to her husband Shemuel. Shemuel wrote to me that she had returned, that one morning she was standing in front of his door, that he had bathed her and put her to bed and that she slept fourteen full hours. I wanted to write him that he must leave Ashkelon because it was a bad place for both of them. Once, as I rode in a darkened bus, I thought I heard Nina's voice. I turned around and no one was there, but it seemed to me that I caught a glimpse of her bright dress and of a white strap shining over her collarbone. Maybe her dress had fallen down over her shoulder, revealing the straps of her brassiere.

Autumn arrived soon after and the clock had to be turned back an hour. All my friends looked forward to the night when they would win a free hour of anarchy, an extra hour of life. For some reason I was afraid of that hour as of an unhealthy growth on the body — a terrible hour of luxury, of Ashkelon. I awoke a bit before the moment when the clock was to be set back. I stood next to the window. Cries for help filled the vacuum of the night, like distress signals from ships at sea. I rolled up my thoughts as if to put them in an empty bottle and set them loose on the wide sea.

At that hour there came a knock on Nina's window. The Roman stood outside, white, smooth, and wonderful like the statue of a god. She followed him to that terrible thicket. There they sat on the trunk of that bent sycamore. Then he drew her with his kisses towards the deserted well house, where the draw chain hung deep into the abyss. She guessed his intention and began to struggle. But he, who had been trained to wrestle from his youth and was nude and greased with wrestler's oil, only laughed. He lifted her and her arms flew upward, as in the ancient sculptures depicting the rape of helpless women. Then he dropped her into the abyss.

The extra hour passed and I closed the window. Next day the radio again began to request help in finding Nina. She had last been seen wearing a white nightgown in the manner of a Greek goddess. After a few days these broadcasts stopped too.

I forgot Nina. But sometimes, I remember her well. First I see her head, then her whole body, her elastic, brown Mediterranean body. They say that sailors first discovered the world was round when they noticed that only the top of a mountain was visible from afar at sea, but that as they approached land, the entire mountain loomed into view. So does Nina rise in the horizon of my memory. First her head, then her entire body. Then I know, like those sailors, that my life too never rests, but revolves and revolves without end.

B. S. Johnson

Instructions
for the Use
of Women
or Here,
You've been Done!

Let me try to set this down with an exactness you may or
may not find curious.

The only point of precision (as distinct from completeness,
to which I feel incapable of aspiring) on which I am un-
decided is the disclosure of her name. This indecision is
principally occasioned by the existence of libel laws of a
surely unnecessarily harsh character: for I am, after all,
only telling the truth as I see it now, remembering to the
best of those faculties I have what I felt reasonably sure
happened at the time. If you are not an acquaintance of
mine (which you are almost certainly pleased not to be) her
name can mean nothing to you; and those who do know me
will already be aware of her name or be easily able, from
their special knowledge, to identify her. So how could she
be harmed? Why should our lawgivers think that she needs
protection?

But in their circumstances I shall call her Winnie, or
Rachel, or Stella, or any other name that reasonably
preserves her gender, as the mood takes me, or rather as
whatever comes to mind at the time a proper name seems

Instructions for the Use of Women

to make the rhythm of the sentence a little less of a failure.
And I shall make unthrifting use of the feminine personal
pronouns. But, whichever, no burden of universality is to be
laid upon the appelative; nor on anything else, either.

I wonder is anyone still reading?

This girl (as she then was) Millie. First eyesetting must
have been at our college, at some time, she was a year or so
behind me, was it two, no, she was in the same year as
Patrick, Neilsen, and all those, the heroic young. A snobby
lot, she told me, at the time I am really writing about,
which was much later, several years after we had both
become post–. I could astound you with an amount of
stunning trivia at this point, if I did not wish to avoid boring
myself. By beginning at the beginning I am doing that,
however, so how about some sex? That I know you will
enjoy: so many commodities sold through sex testify to the
stone certainty of that truth!

At some early point in the post-college period, then, I
must have invited Daphne to count the short rosary of my
balls: one, two, one for luck, three! This must not be misunderstood as a conceited metaphor, but read again, perhaps more carefully. But the invitation went unanswered
for some time, and no speculation can be more likely to
show a slight profit than that this had much to do with a
boyfriend of hers who said he had cancer. More of him
later, if I can be bothered, for I am having enough difficulty
fulfilling my word and getting to the sex soonest as it is.

How to express it?

Ah!

There blew up this very disturbing bubble under my
foreskin (for my parents did not follow the fashionable organ-
scalping of their time, for reasons into which I have never
felt competent enough to inquire). It was after the second (I
think) time that first night, and this bubble I can only
liken to that which can often form, suddenly and almost
remarkably, when a half-fried egg is basted with overheated
fat: something to do with surface tension, perhaps, though I

am no physicist, ha! But my bubble was larger, though perhaps fingering in the dark made it so, or seem so. Obviously it was a blister, but why it should be so large worried me. The cause was almost as obvious: Dora was dry, desiccated, and did not let down her dew, Freda's fanny had not let flow the sweet juices of fornication, Sonya's sluicegates of soft desire had remained shut, Wilhemina's weirwaters had become a wadi of waste land, waste sand – and similar imitations of the euphemisms of the good old prepermissive writers.

But I am the first (and who could challenge that?) to admit that there was another cause, too: I was not (like any of us) as young as I used to be. I was, indeed, as late in the twenties as it was possible to be in those days, and I had been, moreover, (and this may come as a shock) in an unblessed state as regards actual penetration of a female for something approaching four years. Not that, you must understand, I considered myself celibate: like an athlete I had kept the appropriate muscles in fine fettle by regular (for periods, indeed, nightly) exercise. But no, on this occasion it was, I am sure, or feel, the remarkably high friction quotient generated against not an unreceptive (for it was well enough received) but an insufficiently lubricated receptacle for an unusual length of time. This latter point is of major interest (for me, anyway) as this second time, following at who knows (since it was dark) what interval, it took me an unprecedentedly long time to discharge my duty, if such it was, and if not it ought to have been. Indeed, to tell all, I did not go off with that splendid, satisfying *splott* at all, but (the method used being timely withdrawal with Gynomin for additional safety) dissembled by gentle histrionics. I do not know if she was deceived; she gave no sign. For this only I feel guilty about the whole affair: and that only for my own sake, certainly not on account of her. It is the only occasion on which I have found it necessary to feign in this connection.

But the bubble I kept fingering, after the *coitus* had been *interruptus*, being aware of, for a long while, in the dark there. Eventually I fell asleep, and when I awoke it had almost disappeared: though the soreness remained, so there was no dismissing it as a dream, wet or windy, or a nightmare.

I would like it to be borne in mind during the following attempt at description that my appearance too has not been known to cause gasps of admiration or envy, nor to stop traffic in even the less busy streets.

She was a big girl, Harriet, somewhat masculine, I suspected, big except for her breasts, tits, dugs, or mammaries, that is, which somehow protruded less than her stomach, looked at from either side elevation. Yet she did not appear to be fat, exactly, had a waist and good gracile legs. It was her hips, she was very heavy in the hip; I wish I could demonstrate for you with some anatomical model or machinery the heavy, curious articulation of her hips. If I had to sum her up in a cheap phrase, and why I do so when I am under no such compulsion causes me some surprise, I would say she was an incipient trout, a budding if not archetypal trout, even at her age (which at that time was about twenty-five) manifesting distinct troutiness. And ah, again, I would not have you thinking (if you were) that I am envious, or even taking some kind of revenge: for no doubt to her I also was archetypically pisciform, for instance, perhaps clearly seen as as a rock-salmon (dogfish, *Scyllium catulus*), or as the grotesque camerafish, I am a camerafish! No, my only concern, as I have too often said, is to set down what I thought, think, and remember with some exactness. If she wishes she may attempt to do the same: that I allow is her troutish privilege.

Perhaps she was all that I deserved, if in spite of everything there is justice, at that time, and I am very pleased the time is past.

Did you find the bubble bit interesting? I doubt you can have read anything quite like it before. And it is true, however it reads to you. By 'quite like it' I mean anything so curiously comic and uncomic, in just that way. Or perhaps you were embarrassed? In that case it may have been good for you: have you thought of that?

Her character. She had a marked capacity for setness. She would punctiliously leave me to catch a train for no other reason than that she had at some time set her mind on catching that particular train. There was no real reason to go home then, or at all, except the setness, the execution of an arbitrary but pre-determined decision. I thought this was very near to being a mistake, but that is surely natural.

It was a wet summer, poor by popular standards, but popular with me because the number of creepy-crawlies was noticeably diminished. Or perhaps it was just that there were fewer occasions on which I was tempted to sit on the grass.

This was at her flat, in a late Georgian house facing on to Blackheath. She paid a high rent for it, for her. She was a schoolmistress. In the morning she would not let me be seen by the colleague who came to pick her up for school. I watched from an upstairs window, Morris Traveller, woman about forty, and troutlike Doris swinging in her two fine legs, never a romantic glance up at the window of her flat, smiles for the colleague, talking about something from which I was excluded. Do not imagine I did not resent it.

For the rest, or part of the rest, the notes for a failed poem of the time or thereabouts:

Just as though nothing had happened/ Cars still crossed the rain . . . of Blackheath/ Houses proudly primly bowfronted as day night before/ WORMS were stranded across the asphalt paths/ just as they always are by heavy rain?/ a fishmonger laid out stiff mackerel/ ticket office efficient/ the commuters soaked and drily surly/ and the tube so packed as to suggest a grotesque echo of our closeness/ Just as though I had never lost my faith belief/ in loving making love and you had not restored it/

At last, you must be saying, or thinking, rather, the point, or a possible point, at any rate: the unsatisfactoriness of the relationship is being reflected or refracted in what it would be a joke to call the narrative. A suicidal point: make it as unsatisfactory as possible for the reader in order to convey more nearly the point of unsatisfactoriness.

There! A reward for reading this far. Another joke is promised before the end.

There are two ways of taking what has gone so far: your way, and my way. And you are no doubt going to take it your way.

Mind you, in those days I used to be worried about *on to* and *onto*, as well, ha!

Yet I have told you nothing about her, really, Anne, Betty, Celia: nothing that could be shown to you in any meaningful sense to be true. But at least Pyrronism may be true, paradoxically?

Shortly afterwards I met my future wife and lived happily ever afterwards.

I am going to give up this style soon. Perhaps after this. I mean, it is well understood that a man cannot stand still. Change is a condition of life, I remind myself. Perhaps the most admissible one, too.

Nor is this the piece I wanted to write.

But always end with a song and a giggle . . . so sing the following Fescennine joke to yourself:

The usual young man was shipwrecked on a desert island. Fortunately for him he found there others, though only men, who had met with a similar but earlier fate. When he had eaten and drunk of such as the island provided, he felt recovered from his asthenia sufficiently enough to inquire into how this all-male society fared for the other. 'Ah,' said one of his companions-in-distress who recked not of ending sentences with prepositions, 'There we are very well provided for. In the south of the island is exposed at low tide the mouth of a cave at the back of which is a vast store of dried fanny, provenance unknown but highly regarded, and you are most welcome to avail yourself of it as the need takes you.' Our hero was of course at first inclined to regard the fellow as a Barmecide, but, having nothing to lose, soon sought out the delitescent cave and was surprised and pleased to see that the man had indeed been speaking the truth. So, choosing circumspectly from amongst the neatly stacked piles the least hispidulous of those in the front, he was soon enjoying himself with a properly apolaustic fervour. Over the succeeding months and years he came to value this handy dehydrated convenience product so much that when the time came (as it must for the purposes of this anecdote) for the castaways to be rescued he resolved to take back a dozen or so with him: what he had in mind was to produce them triumphantly if any of his acquaintance should accuse him of gasconading, as they naturally might. Jauncing off the boat into the Customs Shed at Falmouth, however, he met with an unexpected setback. 'Anything to declare?' inquired a ventripotent Customs Officer; to which, determined to be truthful, our hero replied: 'Yes. Dried fanny, as a commodity, or, if you prefer the plural, fannies.' The Customs Officer did not laugh, as he found it unsettled people. Instead he expressed a desire to see the objects declared, and was immediately convinced by a glance into the sailor's kitbag. 'How many are there?' he required to know, as though dried fanny were part of the everyday life of the Customs Officer. 'About a dozen,' hazarded the succoured castaway. 'About?' queried the civil servant, 'In that case I'd better count them.' And, licking his enumerating finger, he began to do so. All went well to seven, mere routine, but then he paused, licked his finger again, reflected for a long moment, and said firmly: 'Here, mate, you've been done: this one's an arsehole!'

B. S. Johnson

For Bolocks
Please Read Blocks
Throughout

Fifteen Clonic Conversations for
William Hoyland & Another

A The world is so . . .
B How can you generalize?
A I am fully-paid-up!

*

A The Market is open . . .
B The double pouches on the
  stallholders' women bulge
  and clink, the newcomers
  prod the produce, ices
  remain all the go for the
  dear little ones, bruised fruit
  goes unknowingly home, the
  sun as a special surprise
  sets. . .
A If only I could live without
  buying!
B And selling!

*

A How much?
B How little?

A Small thinker, you think small!

B Gross eater, coarse fisher!

A Bolocks!

B Meunière?

*

A I shall permit myself a quiet smile...

B Oh? Have the neighbours complained about the noisy ones?

*

A The film crew!

B They are our friends!

A Our friends?

B They present our case...

A They are our enemies!

B Our enemies?

A They partialize the totality of our case, they edit *their* view of *our* case.

B *Nothing* can be done.

A Yes, nothing *can* be done!

*

A I haven't been feeling myself lately...

B You want me to do it for you?

*

A This is a genuine Turkish Bath.

B The Turks overran these parts?

A Yes. They were bastards,
then, the Turks.

B We've been bastards
ourselves, in our time.

A Yes. Not now, nor the Turks.

B How come there's still so
much bastardy, then?

A Must be . . . others. . .

B Other who?

A Other Turks. . .

*

A New extensions will increase
the strain. . .

B I was hoping to have mine
painlessly cauterized.

*

A The island looks at its best in
winter. . .

B Faster times are of course
obtained downwind. . .

A Debenham and
Freebody's . . .

B Now and then . . .

A And so forth and so on . . .

*

A You're again in the forefront
of non-stop developments . . .

B It's my nature – don't crucify
me for it!

A I wouldn't crucify you with
someone else's nails!

*

A Why are we here?

B [*laughs uproariously; recovers*]
   The old ones! I love the old
   ones!

A [*savagely*] Have you enjoyed
   sexual congress with your
   mother, then?

*

A How about home?
B Pronounced Hume?
A Yes. *Of the Standard of Taste.*
   'Men of the most confined
   knowledge are able to
   remark a difference of taste in
   the narrow circle of their
   acquaintance, even where the
   persons have been educated
   under the same government,
   and have early imbibed the
   same prejudices. But those
   who can enlarge their view
   to contemplate distant
   nations and remote ages,
   are still more surprised at
   the great inconsistence and
   contrariety. We are apt to
   call *barbarous* whatever
   departs widely from our own
   taste and apprehension; but
   soon find the epithet of
   reproach retorted on us. And
   the highest arrogance and
   self-conceit is at last startled,
   on observing an equal
   assurance on all sides, and
   scruples, amidst such a

contest of sentiment, to
pronounce positively in its
own favour.'

B You mean it doesn't matter
what they think of us?

A No, it doesn't matter; though
it may be painful.

B All is subjective opinion?

A Yes.

B So what does matter?

A Me. And perhaps you.

B Me. And perhaps you!

A Me!

B Me!

A There you are.

B There *you* are!

A Where?

*

A Remedy is none . . .

B Rubbed on by a monk

*

A When did you last learn
anything from what you
really wanted to do?

B I don't understand the
question.

A Neither do I. I was looking to
your answer.

*

A I shall break the rules!

B There are no rules . . .

A I shall invent rules.

B Then *I* shall break *your* rules!

B. S. Johnson

Mean Point of Impact

CONFIRMED 0035 HRS ENEMY OCCUPATION
OF CATHEDRAL SAINT ANSELM 07364219 STOP
AWAIT FURTHER ORDERS BATCOM

Elias was the man John wanted, Elias of Caen who had worked at Amiens and Salisbury, had learnt the subtle lessons of St Denis (where it started) and Chartres, Elias who was still young enough to see a cathedral designed and built and consecrated: to see it done, to have it finished in John's lifetime too.

John's was the initial act of will to build, build, a will sustained through nearly thirty years, and the first exercise of it was in persuading Elias. This he did by trusting the mason's sense of what was now possible and remarkable in architecture, and by offering him as if equal partnership in the project; and he was fortunate, too, in that Elias met and married a woman of the village shortly after he arrived, so that John was able to secure for him the final respect of and position in a narrow community by making him Magister Elias.

> Have care for the comfort of your men, but do not sacrifice atmosphere for comfort.
> Neither atmosphere nor comfort here, in this dark: we might be anywhere, as well be nowhere.

They sank the footings thirty feet until they came to the water table. There were those who said that this was not deep enough, and that they should find another site away from the river where there was bedrock nearer the surface; others that they should build a lighter, smaller structure, even to have no spire at all on the tower; but Elias argued that thirty feet was enough, just enough.

So they outlined the cruciform in trenches, three hundred feet in length and one hundred and eighty across the transepts, and filled them with seventy wagonloads a day of rubble from two quarries and most of the ruins within ten miles or so.

And John stood on a near-by hill and saw the shape of his long cathedral on the ground at last, no longer lines on paper.

Work above ground began first on the nave, and progressed as rapidly as John could have hoped: within eight years it was up to clerestory height, and another five saw it vaulted over. Work on the west front was not far behind, and at the completion of the nave it had been finished up to the height of the string-course just above the great circular window to which Magister Elias had given five anaconcentric thicknesses through to the inner wall: there was no other like it in Europe at the time.

> *Map reference 07364219 . . .*
> *The spire of the Cathedral of St Anselm. . . . Yes.*

Sixteen years after John had first persuaded Elias to build his cathedral there was a fire which severely damaged the partly-built choir and chevet, and which in its wake brought disagreement between Elias and his assistant Nicolas over how they should rebuild. John's will resolved the first problem by raising yet more money from the Crown to offset the loss; and, seeing that Elias's integral conception of the cathedral was being threatened, successfully diverted Nicolas's need and talent for innovation by setting him the Chapter House to design. This he did in the new Decorated Style, with fan vaulting from one slender central column, and with a perfect echo that made the place like an extension of one's skull; but whose acoustics could make heard everywhere an unwary bishop whispering at a Chapter meeting: a light, small-scale foil to the hard strength of the main building.

> *Just south of east, bearing 108° as near as dammit. They'll confirm that from the air, presumably just before dawn.*

The best travelling detailer was an atheist, a wencher, an artist. Elias employed him for his skills, not for his opinions or his morals: because he treated stone honestly, revelled in its own qualities, did not try to make it seem like wood or plaster, exploited stone for what it exactly was. The detailer's mildly ungrateful revenge on his religious patron took the form of a monkey gargoyle which from the choirmaster's room at clerestory level appeared from the back to be hunched over with its hands between its thighs; but from the front it presented a very different aspect. By placing an oval pebble in a runnel so that it alternately held and released water the detailer contrived that during rain the monkey masturbated in passably lifelike spurts. No one except the detailer was ever in a position to see this, he was the only one who ever appreciated and laughed at it: he thought of it as art for his sake. The monkey saluted rain with fertile abandon until the middle of the seventeenth century, when runnel corrosion and wear of the pebble caused a malfunction of the simple mechanism.

> *Range 8,500 yards equals elevation 21–3° on the clinometer.*

Elias had always known of the narrowness of his foundations' loadbearing margin: the certainty that the tower would never carry the spire he had planned came just before his fifty-fifth birthday, but his disappointment was tempered by the realization that he could build to the height he wished, and perhaps even higher, by adoption of Nicolas's Decorated Style for a pierced, hollow spire which would be two thirds or less the weight of a solid one. So Elias and Nicolas worked together in great peace to build a spire that subtly changed its appearance as those on the ground walked past at various distances, being fretted and light and delicately proportionate, the interplay between masonry and space, pierced rondels and finials.

First ranging shot at 8,800 yards . . .

The final act of building was to place at the very top of the spire a casket containing the holy relics of St Anselm together with a tiny fragment of the True Cross. John was ill, and old, but could let no one else perform the ceremony. Bearing the small sealed lead container, he was hauled slowly in a chair up the interior of the spire by the same men on the great treadmill who had raised every stone of its fabric. At the top Elias and Nicolas helped him out through a specially enlarged rondel on to the temporary scaffolding erected round the point of the spire. He shook as he slid the lead casket into place, he turned, looked down, heard voices through the wind, did not look at the others, crawled back towards his chair. Elias followed, Nicolas was left to set mortar on the stone entombing the relics.

. . . second at 8,200 yards . . .

At the consecration the masons shuffled on the enamel, burnt glass tiles. One felt resentful that the clerics now acted as though the building belonged solely to them; worse, were ascribing it to God, not them. A friend spat and said: Let them have it, leave it to them. A third was openly grateful that it had given him a living for twenty years, had enabled him to marry and bring up a family: Where else would I have found such work, he said, for there are no other patrons. It'll be here when those bastards are dead, said another. And their bleeding god, said the first.

. . . observe, split difference, two more ranging shots, observe, split difference, which should then give me the

mean point of impact: the spire of the Cathedral of St Anselm.

John and Elias, old men for their time.
John said: Why do you build?
Elias said: I am a builder . . .
John said: Not for God?
Elias said: I am a builder. I'm not sure about God.
John said: No more am I.
Elias said: Then why have you spent yourself on this house of God?
John said: In order that others shall have a place in which it might seem possible to believe in God.

> *. . . Then commence firing for effect. Impossible to check further, till daylight. Range in any case affected by temperature, wear of gun, strength of propellant, weather, other factors largely unknown, I just fire and hope, it's not a science though they like to make out it is. Try to sleep now.*

By the fifteenth century there was a close; by the sixteenth a small town; by the seventeenth boys of the city evolved an early form of handball against the walls and buttresses of the return to the choir from the Chapter House. The verticals were as plumb as they ever were.

STAND BY BATTERY THREE STOP LAY ON 07364219 BEARING 109° 15′ CHECK VISUALLY FIRST LIGHT THEN COMMENCE FIRING ON ORDER BATCOM

In the latter part of the eighteenth century respect was so far absent that it was found necessary to affix a notice to the eastern wall of the north transept reading DÉFENSE D' URINER; to which within a week was unofficially added SOUS PEINE DE CONFISCATION DE L'OBJET

> *. . . on the bleeding spire, he says, who wants to hit the bleeding spire, what sodding use is that, it's the bleeders*

> *underneath we're supposed to hit, poor sods, though*
> *with all the wear this old cow's seen if we line up on the*
> *bleeding spire we'll be lucky to hit the town let alone the*
> *bleeding church . . .*

An access of piety (or fear about the impossibility of passing a rope through the eye of a needle) in the mid nineteenth century led to very extensive restoration. The flaking, blackened Caen stone was cut back and an ashlar of very similar stone applied. The crockets and finials where damaged were simply squared off and not replaced. Afterwards the cathedral of St Anselm was recognizably the same building, but early twentieth-century *Kunstwissenschaft* was misled into a considerable number of errors.

FIRE!

Biographical Notes

Anthony Burgess

born in Manchester in 1917, was educated at the Xaverian College and Manchester University, where he gained a B.A. in English Language and Literature. In 1940 he joined the army and served at home and abroad, ultimately with the rank of sergeant-major, until 1946. He found time to write poetry but was determined to make his name primarily as a composer. In fact, before abandoning this ambition in 1955, he produced two symphonies, sonatas, concertos for various instruments and popular songs.

After lecturing in England from 1946 to 1954, Burgess went as senior education officer to Malaya where he wrote his first published books. His first main work was a trilogy on the end of British power in the Far East – *The Long Day Wanes*. After Malaya, he went to Borneo as a lecturer, but in 1959 he was invalided home with a suspected brain tumour. He was given a year to live, so, in one year, wrote as many novels as he could – *The Doctor is Sick*, *Inside Mr Enderby*, *The Worm and the Ring*, *The Wanting Seed* and *One Hand Clapping*. The solemn warning of impending death proved groundless. Living in Sussex and London, Burgess produced novels at a slower rate but still with a speed that disconcerted some critics and readers. His chief novels from 1961 until now are: *A Clockwork Orange*, *Honey for the Bears*, *Nothing Like The Sun*, *Tremor of Intent* and *Enderby Outside*.

Burgess has contributed numerous articles and reviews to periodicals at home and abroad and has also written a popular treatise on linguistics, a student's book on the modern novel, a long study of James Joyce, and a shortened version of *Finnegans Wake*.

Susan Hill

born in Scarborough in 1942, wrote her first novel *The Enclosure* when she was seventeen on twenty-five Woolworth's notebooks, and wrote to Pamela Hansford Johnson asking what she should do with it. By the time she was nineteen it had been published, hailed as 'adult' and 'mature', and she had written two plays which were performed at the Belgrade Theatre, Coventry, and another novel, *Do Me a Favour*. After King's College, London, where she read English, she was literary editor of the *Coventry Evening Telegraph* for five years. In 1968, she wrote two novels about old age, *Gentlemen and Ladies* and *A Change for the Better* and in 1969 an outstanding new one about two eleven year old boys, *I'm the King of the Castle*. A book of her short stories, *The Albatross* will be published later this year. She won Arts Council Grants for 1969 and 1970 and now lives in Leamington Spa, working on her new novel and on the libretto for a chamber opera.

Yehuda Amichai

born in Wurtzburg, Germany in 1924, has lived in Israel since the age of twelve. During the war he served with the British Army in the Middle East, after which he joined the Palmach (the shock troops of the Israeli army). After the war of Independence, he studied at the Hebrew University, travelled in England and the United States, and taught in a Jerusalem school. He began to publish poetry in the fifties and his two books of poems have both been published in English. One of them will shortly be published by Penguin.

He has also written a novel *Not Of This Time, Not Of This Place*, published in English in the United States, and has just finished a new novel which he describes as 'grotesque and pornographic'.

B. S. Johnson
born in London in 1933, has written five novels, *Travelling People*, 1963, for which he won the Gregory Award, *Albert Angelo* 1964, *Trawl*, 1966, for which he won the Somerset Maugham Award, *The Unfortunates*, 1969, and a new one, *House Mother Normal*, for publication later this year. He has also published a book of poems, a book of stories and two non-fiction books, *Street Children* and *The Evacuees*. In 1967 he was commissioned to write two plays, *One Sodding Thing After Another* and *Whose Dog Are You?* by the Royal Court Theatre, and in 1968 a film, *You're Human Like The Rest Of Them*, which he wrote and directed, won the Grand Prix at two Short Film Festivals. He has also made two other short films, and a number of documentaries for BBC television. In 1970 he became the first Gregynog Arts Fellow at the University of Wales.

More about Penguins

Penguinews, which appears every month, contains details of all the new books issued by Penguins as they are published. From time to time it is supplemented by *Penguins in Print*, which is a complete list of all books published by Penguins which are in print. (There are well over three thousand of these.)

A specimen copy of *Penguinews* will be sent to you free on request, and you can become a subscriber for the price of the postage. For a year's issues (including the complete lists) please send 25p if you live in the United Kingdom, or 50p if you live elsewhere. Just write to Dept EP, Penguin Books Ltd, Harmondsworth, Middlesex, enclosing a cheque or postal order, and your name will be added to the mailing list.

Some other books published by Penguins are described on the following pages.

Note: *Penguinews* and *Penguins in Print* are not available in the U.S.A. or Canada

Nothing Like the Sun
A Story of Shakespeare's Love-life

Anthony Burgess

Shakespeare had no flash bulbs and no gossip columnists
to contend with. He lived and wrote in an obscurity the
Beatles might well envy.

Yet, with immense ingenuity and gusto, Anthony
Burgess has written a racy, lusty and uninhibited tale of
the poet as a young genius – on the make in life,
in love and in letters.

Not for sale in the U.S.A.

Inside Mr Enderby

Anthony Burgess

'ENGAGED' in the one sure refuge from the ever-predatory female, Mr Enderby locks himself compulsively away in the smallest room, and there closeted he once again scribbles at his poetry in isolated security and release.

On his marriage to a glamorous, wordly-wise widow who carries him off to Rome on their wedding-trip, he is soon convinced that the *dolce vita* is not so much a living but more a way of death.

Not for sale in the U.S.A.

New American Story

Edited by Donald M. Allen and Robert Creeley

William Burroughs, Jack Kerouac, Michael Rumaker, Robert Creeley, William Eastlake, Hubert Selby Jr, Edward Dorn, LeRoi Jones, John Rechy, Douglas Woolf

These seventeen stories dig deep into America today. Each one – whether about a Navaho Indian, queer hustler, or used-car salesman – is an exact refraction of the beliefs, conventions, and behaviour patterns of a people in a state of change.

This change is reflected in the writers' styles. A freedom and individuality new to American writing informs them all – from the explosive 'wordscapes' of Kerouac and Burroughs to the taut power of Robert Creeley and Hubert Selby Jr.

Some of the stories are concerned with a middle-class trapped in a world of advertising and TV; some, the victims of race, perversion, and poverty. Some eschew plot to exploit myth, symbol, and language; many have messages that are hard to take . . .

Penguin Modern Stories

1* William Sansom Jean Rhys David Plante
   Bernard Malamud

2* John Updike Sylvia Plath Emanuel Litvinoff

3† Philip Roth Margaret Drabble Jay Neugeboren
   Giles Gordon

4† Sean O'Faolain Nadine Gordimer Shiva Naipaul
   Isaac Babel

5† Penelope Gilliat Benedict Kiely Andrew Travers
   Anthony Burton

6† Elizabeth Taylor Dan Jacobson Maggie Ross
   Robert Nye

*Not for sale in the U.S.A.
†Not for sale in the U.S.A. or Canada